"It can't be easy being ⟨...⟩t,"

Lucas said softly.

Katie smiled. "I don't think it's ever easy being a parent, single or otherwise. But yeah, being a single mom does present some additional problems."

She met his intense gaze, wishing her heart wasn't beating so fast. "It's been hard being the one who always has to make and enforce the rules. And sometimes it would be nice to just have someone else to bounce things off of, and sometimes it would be nice to just have twenty-four hours…. But no matter how rough it gets, Rusty makes it all worth it."

"Yeah, he is an incredible kid, Katie," Lucas agreed, touched by the depth of her feelings for her child. He reached across the table and covered her hand with his.

He'd been itching to touch her from the moment she'd opened the door to him tonight….

Dear Reader,

Most of us look forward to October for the end-of-the-month treats, but we here at Silhouette Special Edition want you to experience those treats all month long—beginning, this time around, with the next book in our MOST LIKELY TO… series. In *The Pregnancy Project* by Victoria Pade, a woman who's used to getting what she wants, wants a baby. And the man she's earmarked to help her is her arrogant ex-classmate, now a brilliant, if brash, fertility expert.

Popular author Gina Wilkins brings back her acclaimed FAMILY FOUND series with *Adding to the Family,* in which a party girl turned single mother of twins needs help—and her handsome accountant *(accountant?),* a single father himself, is just the one to give it. In *She's Having a Baby,* bestselling author Marie Ferrarella continues her miniseries, THE CAMEO, with this story of a vivacious, single, pregnant woman and her devastatingly handsome—if reserved—next-door neighbor. Special Edition welcomes author Brenda Harlen and her poignant novel *Once and Again,* a heartwarming story of homecoming and second chances. *About the Boy* by Sharon DeVita is the story of a beautiful single mother, a widowed chief of police…and a matchmaking little boy. And Silhouette is thrilled to have *Blindsided* by talented author Leslie LaFoy in our lineup. When a woman who's inherited a hockey team decides that they need the best coach in the business, she applies to a man who thought he'd put his hockey days behind him. But he's been…blindsided!

So enjoy, be safe and come back in November for more. This is my favorite time of year (well, the beginning of it, anyway).

Regards,

Gail Chasan
Senior Editor

Please address questions and book requests to:
Silhouette Reader Service
U.S.: 3010 Walden Ave., P.O. Box 1325, Buffalo, NY 14269
Canadian: P.O. Box 609, Fort Erie, Ont. L2A 5X3

About the Boy

SHARON DE VITA

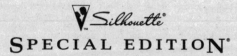

Silhouette®

SPECIAL EDITION®

Published by Silhouette Books

America's Publisher of Contemporary Romance

This one's for the great Chicago police officer,
Sue Hennighan, and her husband, the Sarge, for extending
their hands in kindness, sympathy and friendship and
especially for sharing the antics of their fabulous,
mischievous son, Sean. Make your mom proud, kid!

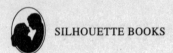 SILHOUETTE BOOKS

ISBN 0-373-24715-X

ABOUT THE BOY

Copyright © 2005 by Sharon De Vita

This edition published by arrangement with Harlequin Books S.A.

® and TM are trademarks of Harlequin Books S.A., used under license.
Trademarks indicated with ® are registered in the United States Patent
and Trademark Office, the Canadian Trade Marks Office and in other
countries.

Visit Silhouette Books at www.eHarlequin.com

Printed in U.S.A.

Books by Sharon De Vita

Silhouette Special Edition

Child of Midnight #1013
*The Lone Ranger #1078
*The Lady and the Sheriff #1103
*All It Takes Is Family #1126
†The Marriage Basket #1307
†The Marriage Promise #1313
††With Family in Mind #1450
††A Family To Come
    Home To #1468
Daddy Patrol #1584
Rightfully His #1656
About the Boy #1715

**Lullabies and Love
†The Blackwell Brothers
††Saddle Falls
*Silver Creek County

Silhouette Romance

Heavenly Match #475
Lady and the Legend #498
Kane and Mabel #545
Baby Makes Three #573
Sherlock's Home #593
Italian Knights #610
Sweet Adeline #693
**On Baby Patrol #1276
**Baby with a Badge #1298
**Baby and the Officer #1316
†The Marriage Badge #1443
††Anything for Her Family #1580
††A Family To Be #1586
My Fair Maggy #1735
Daddy in the Making #1743

Silhouette Books

The Coltons
I Married a Sheik

SHARON De VITA,

a former adjunct professor of literature and communications, is a *USA TODAY* bestselling, award-winning author of numerous works of fiction and nonfiction. Her first novel won a national writing competition for Best Unpublished Romance Novel of 1985. This award-winning book, *Heavenly Match*, was subsequently published by Silhouette in 1985. With over two million copies of her novels in print, Sharon's professional credentials have earned her a place in *Who's Who in American Authors, Editors and Poets* as well as the *International Who's Who of Authors*. In 1987, Sharon was the proud recipient of *Romantic Times*'s Lifetime Achievement Award for Excellence in Writing.

Sharon met her husband while doing research for one of her books. The widowed, recently retired military officer was so wonderful, Sharon decided to marry him after she interviewed him! Sharon and her husband have four grown children, five grandchildren and currently reside in the Southwest.

Lady Louella's Monthly Astrology Newsletter

With summer ending, and fall about to arrive, some challenges and changes are in store for all of us who reside in Cooper's Cove.

As I predicted last month, we now have a new police chief with the retirement of longtime Chief Amos Mayfield, and we also have a new editor of the *Carrier* newspaper, my very own beloved daughter, Katie Murphy.

But beware, children, Mercury will go retrograde early in the month, creating havoc and problems, especially for our newest citizens. So beware and take care as tempers and patience fray. Remember the road to our one true path and our one true partner is not always a smooth or welcome journey.

With a return to school and preparation already under way for the Halloween Festival, it will be a very busy time. But I predict that though the festival will be a joyous success once again, there will be a setback, a major scare that will throw the entire town into an uproar of fear before the situation is finally, successfully resolved.

On a more joyous note, I see two weddings this month. One will be an elopement and a glorious surprise for everyone—including the blushing bride! I'm afraid the other wedding will be a bit rougher going, looking quite bleak before the clouds clear and happiness descends. But as with all things, time, patience, love and understanding will work wonders.

Until next month, wishing you only the brightest stars…Lady Louella

Chapter One

"Lady, I hope you have a *really* good explanation. Or a really good lawyer."

Lucas Porter scowled down at the slender figure kneeling in the dark, apparently digging up his backyard. Even with a full moon, he couldn't see much of her with only the small beam of his flashlight, but he could see enough to know it was a woman.

Although he wanted to get a better look at her, as a cop, common sense had him taking a step back—just in case she was armed—and cursing the fact that he hadn't taken time to grab his gun.

He was lucky he'd grabbed his jeans.

When he'd heard a noise in the yard, he'd just assumed it was a stray animal, so he'd grabbed his flashlight, yanked on his jeans and headed outside to investigate.

In the week since he'd moved to Cooper's Cove and taken over as police chief of the small four-person department, he'd learned pretty quickly that this really was the proverbial small, sleepy little town that was practically a crime-free zone.

But after working undercover for fifteen years in the crime-choked, bustling streets of Chicago, the relative peace, calm and quiet of Cooper's Cove, Wisconsin, had seemed the ideal tonic for all of his ills.

"Lawyer?" the woman repeated absently, not bothering to glance up as she continued to dig, intent on her mission. "Don't be ridiculous. What on earth would I need a lawyer for?"

"Well, how about we start with trespassing, then move right along to say…vandalism?" he asked, going down on his haunches so he was eye level with her, trying hard not to be intrigued by this little bundle of femininity who smelled like heaven, but was apparently short a few buds in her bouquet.

"I'm not vandalizing," she corrected. "Just digging."

"Digging?" he repeated with an absent nod as her scent swirled around him. It was something sweet and sultry, meant to linger in a man's mind like a haunting melody. "Yes, I can see that," he admitted. "But what you call digging, I call vandalizing, not to mention trespassing. And all things considered, trespassing and vandalizing the police chief's backyard in the middle of the night probably wasn't a real smart move."

"Police chief?" The woman chuckled again. "Amos Mayfield has been the police chief of Cooper's Cove for over thirty years and trust me, this isn't his house."

"Amos Mayfield retired over a week ago," Lucas informed his trespasser, and the woman's hands and her gardening spade froze in the dirt.

"Amos Mayfield...*retired?*" she said.

"A week ago," Lucas admitted. "Went to live with one of his daughters," he added conversationally.

Katie Murphy's stomach felt as if it dropped and rolled right over her tennis shoes. She swallowed hard. "And I suppose next you're going to tell me that *you're* the new police chief? And this is *your* house?" she asked weakly, realizing the man was probably sizing her up for a straightjacket. Or a jail cell.

Good grief! Katie's eyes slid closed and she wished she could just disappear into the hole she'd just dug.

"Look, I'm really sorry," she stammered, shoving her hair out of her face and trying to smile. "I uh...know... know how this looks, but—"

"Trust me, you don't," he insisted. "I'm Lucas Porter, chief of the Cooper's Cove Police Department." He extended his hand and Katie looked down at her own hands, filthy with dirt. She wiped them down her jean shorts before taking his hand and allowing him to help her up. Instinctively, her hand warmed and tingled from his touch and it totally unnerved and distracted her since she'd hadn't felt that kind of sizzle from someone's touch in years.

"Now that we know who I am, how about you tell me who you are?" he asked, a glint of humor in his eyes as he studied her.

"You mean besides Cooper's Cove resident lunatic?" she asked, shoving her tangled hair out of her face again as he nodded. "I'm…I'm uh…Katie Murphy, Lady Louella's daughter." Nervous, Katie rubbed her dirty hands up and down her shorts, wondering how she was going to explain to her son that she'd spent their first night home in Cooper's Cove—in a jail cell.

Well, maybe if she talked fast and explained the situation she might be able to talk her way out of this. Hey, it always worked for her mother, she might as well give it a shot.

"This was my mother's house before she sold it to you. Before she sold it she was supposed to retrieve something from the backyard, something that belongs to my eleven-year-old son Rusty, something he and his dad planted in the backyard a few years ago." Almost breathless, she rushed on. "But my mom forgot, so that's why I'm here in the middle of the night, trespassing and digging up your—"

"Wait." Confused, Lucas held up his hand. "Take a breath here, Katie," he said with a laugh. "Because you are making me seriously dizzy." He hesitated for a moment, trying to put the pieces together. "Lady Louella is your *mother?*" He went from confused to surprised in a split second. "Lady Louella, that sweet little woman who runs the Astrology Parlor down on Main Street and sold me this house is your *mother?*" He simply stared at her. "*You're* little Katherine?"

"Afraid so," Katie admitted with a small smile and a shrug. "But I'm a little old to be called little Katherine, don't you think?" Her smile widened. "I much prefer Katie."

He nodded, too stunned to do much else. He was

having a hard time reconciling the headstrong, mischievous little girl Lady Louella constantly talked about with the gorgeous woman standing in front of him.

Wanting to get a better look at her, Lucas stepped closer. The yellow halogen light from the alley cast a long, soft shadow over the yard—and her.

The skintight, threadbare jean shorts she had on hugged her butt and waist like Saran Wrap, and her thin cotton top, which was a shade of peach that only made her fair skin seem more translucent, hinted at the delicate curves beneath.

Her hair was a mass of red, gold and auburn curls that fell to her shoulders, cascading around a face that was nothing short of breathtaking. Pale, delicate skin, big curious green eyes, and a faintly full bow mouth had Lucas wanting to swipe his suddenly damp hands down his jeans.

He had to admit little Katherine was stunning. She had the kind of looks that made a man feel as if he'd been blindsided by a right hook.

He realized with a start that he felt something he never thought he'd feel again. Lust. Pure, unadulterated lust, and it threw him off balance simply because he was certain he'd buried those kinds of feelings when he'd buried his wife, along with his son, two years ago.

The feelings, the stark awareness of this woman and everything about her, was arousing a whole host of emotions he'd long thought buried, emotions he no longer *allowed* himself to feel.

She shifted and he caught another hint of her lush, feminine scent, and it immediately distracted him again. Keeping a steel band tightly around his emotions the past two years had not been a hardship, at least not until this moment.

And the fact that this woman had made him *feel* something—something he thought himself immune from—instantly made him wary of her.

Trying to shake off his feelings, Lucas looked at her carefully, trying to get his thoughts in order. "Now what's this about your mother burying something—"

"No, not my mother," she corrected, then sighed. "My late husband, Jed. He was a pilot in the National Guard, and five years ago, shortly before he left for his annual two weeks of active duty, he and my son Rusty buried a time capsule in the backyard. See, Jed was going to be gone for Rusty's first day of school, and he felt terrible about it, so the two of them decided to do a sort of a special father-son project to kind of make up for Jed not being here on such an important day."

"Okay, I got it so far," Lucas said with a nod, remembering how excited his own son had been on the first day of school. It was a bittersweet memory, and immediately jolted Lucas's heart when he realized there would be no more "firsts" in his son's life. The pain came hot and fast, spearing his heart and leaving it aching in a very familiar way.

"Anyway, Rusty and Jed planted this time capsule, and they'd made plans to retrieve it when Jed came home two weeks later."

Lucas nodded. "Okay, I got that much." He hesitated, still trying to put the pieces together, then he looked at her carefully and saw the haunting sadness in her eyes. He recognized it simply because he saw the same look in his own mirror every morning. "But your husband didn't come home, did he?" he asked quietly, realizing she'd said *late* husband.

"Jed's engine malfunctioned during maneuvers in the mountains. His copter crashed, killing everyone on board."

"I'm so sorry," Lucas said, feeling helpless to offer more. He wished he could tell her he knew how she felt, because he, too, had lost his spouse as well as his son. But he hadn't actually been able to talk about them aloud yet, even though it had been almost two years.

The wound and the ever present guilt that his family was dead and he was alive was still too new, too fresh, and far too painful. He didn't know if he'd ever be ready to talk about what had happened.

"Thanks. Anyway, to make a long story longer, last winter my mom had a slight stroke and couldn't take the stairs in this house any longer, so she moved in with my Aunt Gracie and decided to sell the house." Katie shrugged. "When my mom sold the house, she completely forgot about Rusty's time capsule."

"So…what?" Lucas asked with a frown. "You just remembered the time capsule today and decided to wait until the middle of the night to come dig it up?"

"Well, yes. And no," she admitted with a laugh, seemingly realizing how ludicrous this really sounded.

"Well that certainly clarifies things," he admitted with an amused smile.

"Rusty and I just moved back to Cooper's Cove today. We bought a house here and tomorrow we move

in, and I'd promised him he could bury his treasure box
in our backyard, but—"

"Why didn't you just buy this house?" Lucas asked
more out of curiosity than anything else, glancing at the
two-story white clapboard he now owned. It really was
too big for one person, and clearly it was a family home,
but he'd fallen in love with it the moment he'd walked
inside of it, maybe because of the family feeling he got
whenever he'd entered it.

"I can't take the steps, either," Katie admitted. "I've
got a bum knee. Old track injury that makes daily steps
an impossibility."

"Okay, got it," he said with a nod. "So you and your
son bought your own house—"

"Right, and tomorrow when we move in, Rusty's
going to want his time capsule so he can bury it in our
own backyard, but since my mom forgot about it, she
asked me to come retrieve it before Rusty realized she'd
forgotten something so precious to him."

"Okay." Lucas nodded, realizing this story was too
far-fetched not to be the truth. But the cop in him
knew he'd better ask a few more questions, check her
and her story out a bit more—just to be on the safe
side. "You said you and your son just returned to
Cooper's Cove?"

"That's right," Katie said. We've been living in Madison for a little over five years, since shortly after Jed
died." She shrugged. "Jed and I met when I was in first
grade, we were sweethearts all through school and married two weeks after my high school graduation so I
never had a chance to go to college. Once he was killed,

I realized I had to go back to school if I wanted to be able to properly support myself and my son."

"That's understandable."

"Rusty and I moved to Madison so I could attend the state university. I graduated with a degree in journalism, and took a job with the *Madison Free Press* in order to get some experience before returning home here to take over the *Cooper's Cove Carrier.*"

"You're a *reporter?*" Lucas said slowly as everything inside of him stilled. Reporters had made his life a nightmare after his wife and son had been killed, hounding him, his friends and his colleagues in an effort to get any tidbit of information, sensationalizing the story and his personal tragedy for their own profit.

There seemed to be nowhere he could run, nowhere he could hide to get away from the media's endless questions and prying eyes. And the experience had left a very bitter taste in his mouth for the press and their unscrupulous tactics.

"Actually, I'm not just a reporter, but also the new managing editor," Katie said with pride. "The *Cooper's Cove Carrier* has been in my dad's family for generations." Cocking her head, she realized Lucas's face had changed, darkened, and suspicion glinted in his eyes. It immediately put her back up. "Something about reporters you don't like?" she asked, deliberately keeping her tone light.

He hesitated for a moment. "I can think of a lot more important ways to make a living than snooping into other people's lives," he said very slowly, unable to conceal his disdain.

"Snooping?" she repeated, indignant at his words and tone. Katie slapped her hands to her slender hips, her gaze challenging. "Is that what you think I was doing here tonight? *Snooping on you?"* She glared up at him, stunned by his audacity.

"I don't know," he said quietly, his natural suspicions about reporters kicking in. "Why don't you tell me?"

Temper simmering, Katie took a step closer to him, not caring that he towered over her. "I *told* you what I was doing here," she said tightly. "Now you can believe me or not. Quite frankly I'm too tired to care. But, for the record, I don't go around snooping into other people's lives or their business, nor do I do my investigating by sneaking around in the middle of the night. I'm a professional, and pride myself on doing my job with character and integrity, and I expect to be treated with the same courtesy you'd treat any other professional, whether you like my profession or not."

Coming home hadn't just been a decision, but a carefully planned *destination* that had taken her almost six long years of hardship and worry to accomplish. She'd worked too hard and too long to have someone disparage her or her occupation just because of some preconceived notion or opinion.

Furious, she glared up at him. "Now, are you going to arrest me or what?" she demanded. The moment the words were out, her mouth snapped shut in horror.

Good grief! She'd just given this guy permission to *arrest* her! Katie wanted to groan. She didn't do rash or reckless—that was her mother's arena. She was always calm. She was always rational. She was *always* utterly reasonable.

Until she'd come face-to-face with this man.

He was standing so close to her, she could all but feel his body heat trying to draw her in. If it wouldn't have seemed downright rude, she would have taken a couple of steps back and away from him just to put some distance between them.

There was *something* about this guy—a slow, intense maleness that made her feel as if her skin was just a tad too tight. And it was throwing her off balance.

She glanced up at him and felt her heart skip a beat. He was tall, towering over her five-foot-three frame, and unbelievably put together, with chiseled muscles, lean hips and long, lanky legs.

His hair was an inky black that spilled over his forehead. His eyes were big and blue, and held a hint of sadness, she realized as she studied him.

His face was a slash of masculine planes and angles that looked like it had been sculptured together by a wildly sensuous artist. And then there was his mouth, Katie thought with a soft sigh. It was soft, full and made her silently wonder if his mouth was as wonderful as it looked.

The combination was enough to give him the kind of looks that would make a woman—any woman—take a long, second look as soon as she stopped drooling. Or babbling, as in Katie's case.

So he was gorgeous. She'd seen gorgeous men before and had never reacted like this.

Men didn't put her on edge, or make her feel this

way, at least not anymore, simply because since her husband's death, she'd treated all men like affectionate big brothers. It made life, at least her life as a woman, so much simpler.

Until now.

"Are you going to arrest me?" Katie asked meekly, all but holding her breath.

"Why don't we just go with the 'or what' scenario?" Lucas answered. "It's late, we're both tired, and a little testy," he added. He lifted a hand to stop whatever barrage of words she was about to launch at him. "Why don't you let me take you home?"

"But—"

He pressed a finger to his lips and the action instantly snapped her mouth closed again. "I'll drive you home," he continued quietly, "and then I'll come back and retrieve Rusty's time capsule and have it back to you in the morning before he even wakes up."

He didn't want her to think he was totally heartless, but he wanted her away from him so he could retreat behind the solitary wall of grief he'd built for himself, a wall he'd allowed no one to penetrate.

At least not until tonight.

Until he'd run into her.

Shaking the thoughts away, Lucas glanced around, realizing it would be best if he just got rid of her.

He managed a small smile. "It's late and from what I've learned about Cooper's Cove, I figure within about four minutes tops, one of my neighbors is going to come wandering over to see what the commotion is about, and I don't think either of us wants to explain why the new managing editor of the town newspaper was caught digging up the police chief's backyard in the middle of the night." His smile widened when she groaned. "And then of course, we'll have to face the fact that news of our midnight escapade will be all over town—an exaggerated version, of course—before either of us has our coffee in the morning."

"You're right," Katie admitted with another groan. The last thing she wanted was to become the subject of town gossip before she'd even unpacked. "If you wouldn't mind returning Rusty's time capsule in the morning, I'd sincerely appreciate it," she said.

"I don't mind. Just let me go in and get my shoes and my car keys and then I'll take you home."

Katie nodded. "Fine. I'll wait here."

She watched him disappear into the house, wondering what it was about this man that had her responding to him like a schoolgirl with a runaway mouth?

Leveling her chin in the darkness, Katie took a slow, deep breath to try to get back some control. It didn't matter what this man stirred in her, or what he thought of her, she reasoned. She had far too many responsibilities to even consider allowing a man—any man—into her life. Or her son's. And they were a package deal.

She'd never risk having Rusty's heart shattered again. Once in a lifetime was more than enough—and Rusty's heart *had* been shattered by his father's sudden death, as had hers, and that was more than enough grief and pain for one lifetime for both of them.

She had her responsibilities to her son, her aging

mother and her new demanding job. There was no time or room for anything else in her busy life, especially a man.

She'd been doing fine on her own for the past six years, and fine and alone was exactly how she intended to proceed into the future.

"All set?" she asked, as Lucas came out the back door and quietly shut it behind him.

He held up his keys in answer as he started toward her, his gaze on hers.

Nervous and needing to say something as he got closer, she decided to apologize, since he was, after all, the new police chief and she had dug up his backyard.

"Look, I really am sorry about all of this. I never would have intruded on your privacy had I known you were already living here. My mother told me the new owner wasn't moving in until next week, so I figured I'd be safe." She shrugged. Her mother's astrology charts had been off—again. She'd assured Katie that the new owner wasn't moving in until the next full moon, which wasn't supposed to be until next week. Katie glanced up at the sky and had to smile at the bright, blazing full moon beaming down at her.

"This was truly an honest mistake, and…and…I… don't know what else to say except I'm sorry."

He chuckled, surprising her. "Now why do I have a feeling that's a first?"

She looked up at him, confused. "What's a first?"

"That you don't know what else to say?" He laughed at her expression, then took her elbow as he guided her toward the back gate.

Katie froze, as did Lucas. The brush of his skin on

hers—warm, alive and very, very male—sent an unwelcoming rush of desire racing through her, nearly knocking her off balance.

Her panicked gaze flew to his and she saw a momentary flash of desire, just as strong, powerful and urgent as her own, but those feelings were quickly replaced by such raw, unbearable pain it almost made her knees weak.

She had no idea what had caused Lucas's pain. She only knew she recognized it because she'd felt it—saw it in herself for a very long time after her husband's death. And it touched something deep inside her wounded heart, something she'd thought protected and hidden from the world.

Seemingly realizing they'd both felt something strong and powerful, Lucas released her arm, then avoided her gaze. "My…uh…car's parked in the garage."

Nodding silently, Katie wrapped her chilled arms around herself and followed Lucas toward the back gate.

She had no idea what had just happened between them, but she knew she couldn't let it happen again, couldn't afford to allow herself to respond to this man in any way.

So she decided to tackle this problem in the same calm, reasonable way she tackled any other problem she confronted.

She'd simply avoid the man.

If she couldn't avoid the feelings he raised in her, then the only solution was to avoid *him*.

And since she didn't plan on digging up his backyard again, Katie was pretty confident she wouldn't have to worry about seeing Lucas Porter anytime soon.

Chapter Two

Shortly before dawn the next morning, Lucas let himself out of his house, and headed toward his garage with Katie's gardening spade and Rusty's time capsule box in tow. He'd promised Katie he'd have the box back to her before Rusty woke up this morning, and he honored his promises, especially when they concerned a little boy.

As he drove through the quiet little town, the sun was just spilling light over the horizon. Most residents were still sleeping, but for him, sleep had become an elusive companion ever since his wife's and son's deaths. He spent more time each night tossing and turning than sleeping.

Every time he closed his eyes an image of his burning car filled his mind's eye, tormenting him, making sleep impossible. Even after all this time, he could still see the images clearly, as if they'd just happened yesterday.

It had been a typical frigid winter morning in Chicago. They'd all overslept and his son Todd had missed the school bus. His wife Brenda's car wouldn't start, so she'd taken his car, intending to drive their son to school and be back in time for Lucas to leave for work.

He'd been working undercover on a gang-related drug case for almost a year—a year that his wife spent worrying, begging him to transfer out of gang crimes, fearing it was just too dangerous. But he'd refused, determined to do something to stop the drug suppliers who were filling the streets and the schools with their poisons, putting even young kids like his eight-year-old son at risk.

He'd still been in bed that fateful morning, snuggled beneath the warmth of the covers when he'd heard the explosion. It rocked him and the entire house. By the time he'd raced outside, it was too late. The car was in flames. His family dead from a car bomb meant for him.

He didn't remember much of those first, grief-filled months, except that the department had confirmed the bomb had been meant for him, planted no doubt by the drug dealer he'd been trying to bring down. Somehow, his cover had been blown, and his family had paid the ultimate price.

The press went on a feeding frenzy, and he desperately tried to elude them. It had both sickened and disgusted him that the press tried to exploit and capitalize on his personal tragedy, simply for headlines.

Fed up and furious at the constant intrusion into his life, he'd finally transferred to another police district, hoping to end the nightmare, but one night, he and his new partner had driven to meet a snitch, not knowing an eager reporter had tailed them. When the reporter had gotten out of her car to follow them, calling out Lucas's name, she'd blown his cover. The perpetrator they were meeting panicked and started shooting, grazing his partner in the leg.

That was the final straw. At the end of his emotional rope, Lucas realized if he ever wanted to get any peace, if he ever wanted to try to put the pieces of his life back together, he had no choice but to resign from the police force and move since it was the only way to shake the press.

Those had been very dark days for him, he recalled, and he knew without his job, without his family, there was no reason to stay in Chicago, so he decided to move to his family's cabin along Cooper's Cove Lake.

As a kid, his family had spent every summer at their cabin in Wisconsin. Now that his parents were gone, the cabin had passed to him and his three brothers, and it seemed the perfect place to try to recover from his grief and put what was left of his life back together.

At first, both had seemed impossible. How could he ever forgive himself for putting his family in danger? They'd died because of a bomb meant for him and there was no getting away from the guilt or the shock. He knew he'd never again be able to risk his heart, never again love anyone simply because doing so put anyone he loved in far too much danger. And if a loved one was in danger, then it left him vulnerable—vulnerable to the horrific pain and loss that had eaten away at his heart.

He'd barely survived the loss and heartbreak the first time, and he wasn't certain he would survive a second time. So he'd buried his heart behind a steel fortress, intending to never risk loving someone else.

In time, he realized he needed to go back to work, not just for the income, but he needed something to fill his time and occupy his mind. Being a cop wasn't just *what* he did, but *who* he was, and he needed to find some semblance of himself again.

During their family's summers in Cooper's Cove, Lucas's dad had become friendly with just about everyone, so when Amos Mayfield, an old fishing buddy of his dad's, asked to see Lucas one afternoon, he never anticipated that Amos was about to retire, and wanted Lucas to take over as the chief of the Cooper's Cove police department.

After some serious soul-searching, he realized maybe this was just what he needed. He could go back to doing what he did best—being a cop, without worrying about big-city crime or the press dogging his steps. So he'd moved from the cabin, bought a house in town and now was trying to make a new life for himself.

And he thought he'd been doing a fairly good job until he'd run into Katie Murphy.

Just the thought of her brought an unwelcome smile. There was something about that woman, he realized, something he just couldn't put his finger on, something that was infectiously alive.

And only someone who'd felt dead for a very long time could appreciate that quality, he decided, as he pulled up to her mother's house.

After parking his car, Lucas headed toward the back porch, intending to simply drop her stuff off and leave. But, after setting Katie's things on an old picnic table, he was just about to start back down the stairs again when someone called his name.

"Lucas? Is that you, dear?" Clad in a blue satin robe, Katie's mother stood framed in the open back door, a smile on her face, a large mug of coffee in her hand.

"Yes, ma'am," he said with a smile, turning around and heading back up the steps. He always got such a kick out of Lady Louella and her supposedly psychic, equally vivacious younger sister, Gracie. The first thing he'd asked the day they met was why she was called Lady Louella.

She merely stared at him and responded, "Well, why not?" She'd laughed at his surprise, patted his arm and assured him it was merely to give her astrology parlor some color and authenticity.

Now, Louella beamed at him. "I was just about to call you to report a prowler."

"Nope, not a prowler," he said with a sheepish grin. "Just me. I'm sorry if I startled you. I just came by to drop something off for Katie," he said, motioning toward the time capsule.

"Oh, Lucas, thank you." Louella's eyes misted and she pressed a hand to her heart. "I can't tell you how much this means to me and to Katie." She beamed at him again as she scooped the box in her arms. "Well as long as you came all this way, the least I can do is offer you a cup of coffee." Without giving him a chance to answer, she opened the back door. "Come along now, I might even be able to find a piece of my homemade pound cake for you."

He was sitting at the kitchen table, just finishing a piece of Louella's amazing pound cake, when Katie walked in.

"Mother?" Katie came to a stop, staring at Lucas in shock. He was the last person she expected to see this morning.

Her breath seemed to back up in her throat at the mere sight of him. In full light, she could see that the man was just as breathtakingly gorgeous as she'd thought.

"Cow cakes," Katie muttered under her breath, stealing her son's favorite expression. At the moment, her life would be much easier if Lucas was short, pudgy and ugly.

He'd haunted her mind all night, so she didn't get much sleep, which had left her feeling tired, restless and just a bit cranky.

"Good morning, dear," her mother said with a smile.

"Morning," Katie returned grumpily.

What was the man doing here, sitting at her mother's kitchen table at the crack of dawn as if it was the most natural thing in the world?

She looked at Lucas again and felt a slow warmth unfurl inside her belly, a warmth that both amazed and terrified her. Amazed her because she was certain she was immune to such feelings, and terrified because she knew she couldn't *afford* such feelings.

Disgusted that she hadn't merely imagined the impact he'd had on her, Katie's grumpiness increased.

"Pour yourself some coffee, dear," Louella instructed, as if having a gorgeous man at her breakfast table at the crack of dawn was an everyday occurrence. "Lucas and I are just reminiscing about last week's seniors' dance. The senior dances are always so much fun, but the women far outnumber the men, something we're going to have to try to correct." She brightened suddenly. "Lucas, as police chief, maybe you can enlist some more of the single men to attend. I mean surely being police chief has some perks," she said delicately, cocking her head to look at him. "What do you think?"

Realizing the man was totally perplexed by her mother, Katie's laugh was quick and easy. "What my mother basically just asked you, Lucas, was if you'd mind if she *conned* you into using your position as police chief to strong-arm single, suitable men to attend the next seniors' dance." Katie grinned as she poured herself some coffee and self-consciously tightened the sash on her robe before turning back to Lucas and her mother. "Isn't that right, Mother?"

Louella flushed. "Well, dear, I don't know that I would have used the word...*conned,*" she admitted sheepishly, then grinned at Lucas. "But, I suppose it will do." Mischief danced in her eyes. "So what do you think, dear?"

Realizing he had indeed just been very politely conned, Lucas couldn't help but laugh as well. "Tell you what, Louella, how about if I see what I can do? I'm sure I should be able to corral some single men to serve as escorts for that dance every month."

"Thank you, Lucas. I knew we could count on you." Louella drained her cup, then stood up. "I'm sorry, children, but it's getting late and I've got to go get dressed and open the shop. Aunt Gracie's already gone. She had a doctor's appointment early this morning." Frowning a bit, Louella turned to Katie. "Now, dear, you're sure you don't need any help with the movers today?"

"No, Mom. Honest. Everything's under control. Rusty's starting school this morning and I'm going into the paper. The movers won't be here until later this afternoon, and then Rusty and I plan to spend the evening unpacking and getting settled."

"Very well, dear, but if you change your mind, Aunt Gracie and I will be at the shop until three as usual. Just call if you need anything. And don't worry, I'll be home before Rusty gets home from school." Smiling, Louella bent to kiss Lucas's cheek. "Thank you for returning Rusty's box. And next week we'll talk about the Halloween carnival and the seniors' booth." Her eyes gleamed as she patted his shoulder. "I'm thinking of having a kissing booth this year. But we'll chat about that later."

"Kissing booth?" Lucas repeated with a lift of his brow after Louella had left, and Katie laughed again, warmed in spite of herself by the way he'd treated her mother.

"She's got your number, Lucas, and apparently intends to call it whenever the mood strikes. So be forewarned," she said, realizing a man who was so kind to her mother could quickly score a lot of points with her. "You just may find yourself the main attraction at the seniors' kissing booth at the Halloween festival this year."

Lucas swallowed hard. "Main attraction?" he said, barely able to conceal a shudder. "Kissing booth? I think I'll have to think about that one for a while."

"Sounds like a good idea. But let me warn you, small towns have a way of becoming smaller the longer you live in them."

"I know," he admitted with a smile. "The mayor's already given me the lecture about how living in a small town is all about individual participation and community spirit. He even got me to sign up for the new Buddy program."

"Buddy program?" Katie repeated, still leaning against the counter. She didn't want to get any closer to him, as it was, having him in the kitchen made her feel incredibly nervous and self-conscious, to say nothing about what it was doing to her poor heart.

Lucas nodded. "It's a new mentor program the town council came up with to provide a male mentor for fatherless boys. Apparently we've got quite a few boys without fathers and quite a few men who are childless or else retired whose children are long gone. Most of these guys are alone and lonely, with plenty of time and skills on their hands. So the mayor thought if we paired some of them up to mentor fatherless boys it would benefit both." Lucas smiled. "The mayor just wants to make certain he's taking care of everyone's needs and he thought this Buddy for a Boy program was a good idea."

"Sounds like it's an election year," Katie said with a chuckle. Her gaze met his and froze, and for a split second there was an electrified silence between them.

"Well, it's getting late," Lucas said, draining his coffee cup and getting to his feet. "I just wanted to make certain you got Rusty's time capsule."

Katie glanced at her son's beloved box sitting on the counter and felt a small, sad ache at the memories that rushed over her. The memories were an instant reminder of why she couldn't afford to risk her heart. Or respond to this man, no matter what he made her feel.

"Thank you, Lucas. I really and truly appreciate it. And I know Rusty will, too," she added softly.

He took a step closer to her. "You're welcome," he said.

For a moment, they merely stood there, neither moving nor speaking. Katie lifted a hand to her throat, hoping it would ease the sudden pressure building that made it nearly impossible to breathe.

Lucas watched her, then slowly lifted a hand and brushed a stray strand of hair from her cheek.

"Lucas, I—" Her eyes slid closed as she tried to gather herself. His touch, so brief, so gentle, sent a shiver through her and touched every single female nerve ending, reminding her just how long it had been since she'd been touched, held, or comforted by a man.

"Ma?" Rusty's voice echoed through the house, startling her out of her reverie. "Are you up yet?"

"In the kitchen," she called back, smiling at the sound of her son's voice. It broke the tension between her and Lucas. "Obviously that's my son."

Lucas chuckled. "So I gathered." He hesitated a brief moment. "I'd better go. You've got a busy day and I've got to get to the office. Thank your mom for the coffee." He turned and headed toward the back door, pausing to turn back to her for a moment. "And by the way, Katie, if you need any help with heavy lifting or moving today, just give me a call." His smile was slow and devastating. "I've got a pretty strong back and plenty of time."

"Thank you," she said, surprised and touched by his generous offer.

"See you," Lucas said as he headed out the door.

Still shaken, Katie merely stood there, absently patting her heart to calm it down, as she silently stared after him. Oh yeah, she'd be calling him for help *real* soon, she thought dully. She was trying to stay away from the man, not become his new best friend!

Realizing she was probably overreacting, Katie sighed, then finished her coffee. Now that Lucas was out of sight, maybe—just maybe—she could finally get the blasted man out of her mind.

"Hey, Ma?" Rusty asked a few minutes later as he raced into the kitchen. At eleven, he was a tall, reedy ball of energy, with a mop of rust-colored curls, a face full of freckles and a pair of sea-green eyes that always seemed to be filled with mischief. "Can I ride my bike to Sean's after school?" he blurted, all but dancing with each word.

"Did you guys ask Sean's mother about this?" Katie asked with a lift of her brow.

"'Course," he assured her with a grin.

Sean Hennighan and Rusty had been friends since they were toddlers. Now that Katie and Rusty had returned to Cooper's Cove for good, the boys had simply picked up their friendship right where they'd left off.

"Okay, but did you forget the movers are coming today?" Katie asked.

"Nah, I didn't forget," Rusty said, scuffing the toe of his new gym shoes on the floor. "But I thought maybe I could go by Sean's for just a little while first?" Huge green eyes pleaded with Katie. "Sean's got a brand new Xbox and he said maybe I could try it. It's just so totally cool. So can I go? Huh? Can I?"

"And what about the unpacking?" she asked, watching the excitement dim in his eyes.

"I forgot," he muttered dejectedly. "Cow cakes," he mumbled under his breath.

"How about if we make a deal? You can go to Sean's for an hour and a half," Katie compromised. "But you have to promise to come home from Sean's right on time since Grandma will be waiting for you, and then help me unpack tonight *without* complaining. Is it a deal?"

"Deal." Eyes shining, his grin widened. "Thanks, Ma."

"You're welcome." She smiled, then draped an arm around his slender shoulders. "I've got something for you, Rusty." Reaching for his time capsule with her free hand, Katie hesitated, not quite knowing how he'd respond. "Do you remember when you and Daddy planted this in Grandma's backyard?"

He'd only been six when his father had died, and yet, they'd been so unbelievably close, she was certain most of Rusty's memories of his father were intact. At least she hoped so, for her son's sake.

Her worries dissolved as his eyes widened, looking

at the time capsule box. She saw the quick glistening of tears before he quickly blinked them away.

"Yeah. It's my time capsule treasure box," he said, reaching out and taking the box from her. "Dad and I buried it right before he left." Rusty stared at it for a moment, reverently running a hand gently across the top. "We were supposed to dig it up together when Daddy came home," he added quietly.

"That's right," Katie said, reaching out to lay a hand on his cheek, needing to just touch him. "Well, honey, I promised you when we finally moved into our very own house you could plant it in our backyard, and since we're moving into our own house today I thought you might like to…you know…" Shrugging, Katie let her voice trail off as she watched a myriad of expressions race across her son's freckled face, her own heart aching for him.

Rusty merely stood there for a moment, still and quiet for a change before lifting his gaze to hers. "Ma?"

"Yes, honey?"

"Uh…uh…do you think it would be okay if I…uh… just kept this in my new room for a little while?" Shuffling his feet, he rushed on. "You know so I could maybe just…look at it and stuff?"

She smiled. "Of course, sweetheart."

"I'll bury it in our backyard later, but for now, I'd just like to keep it in my new room so I could…like, see it once in a while." He glanced up at her. "Is that okay?"

"Of course, honey. We can make a special place for it on top of your bookcase. What do you think?"

"Cool," he said with a grin. He glanced down at the

box again, touching the top. "Ma, do you think…do you think Dad…uh…misses me?"

"Oh, sweetheart." Katie reached for Rusty, dragging him close to hug. "Of course Daddy misses you, as much as you miss him I'm sure," she said, resting her head gently atop his head. He was growing so fast, pretty soon he'd be taller than her. With a sigh, she drew back to look at him. "Do you remember what I've always told you?" She lifted his chin so she could look into his eyes. "That daddy was always with you, every day, no matter where you went, or what you did?" She laid a hand over his heart. "Daddy's right here, always, in your heart."

His lower lip was trembling, but Rusty nodded. "Do you remember when I was little?" he asked. "And I used to cry because I missed Dad? And you told me that anytime I wanted to talk to Dad I could just…like, talk to him, and that he'd always hear me?"

"I remember, honey."

A sheepish grin flashed as he looked up at her. "Sometimes Ma, sometimes I still do…talk to Dad, I mean."

Chuckling softly, she gave him a quick squeeze. "Well honey, let me tell you a secret. I'm much older than you—"

"No kidding," he quipped with a lightning grin, giving her a gentle poke with his elbow.

"Hey," she protested, giving him a quick affectionate bump back with her hip. "I'm not that old," she said. "Anyway, my dad's been gone since I was just ten years old, and as old as I am now sometimes I still talk to him."

"Really?" Astonished at the idea, Rusty's eyes widened. "You still talk to your dad?"

"Yeah, honey," she said with a wistful sigh. "Sometimes I still do. I still miss my father every day of my life," she admitted, blinking back sudden tears. "When you love someone you never stop missing them, especially a parent. And a parent never stops missing their child. Never. That's why I know Daddy is always with you, watching over you."

"'Cuz he loved me and stuff?" Rusty asked, and Katie nodded.

"More than anything in the world."

She hesitated, wanting to assure him that however he needed to deal with his feelings about his dad, it was all right. There was no right way or wrong way. Only the way that gave him comfort.

"Rusty, honey, there's a very special bond between kids and their moms and dads, a bond that nothing can ever break, no matter how old either of them gets. Not even death. That unbreakable bond is always there. So don't ever forget that. Daddy's always with you. In your heart, safe and protected and connected to you on every level. And you can talk to him anytime you want."

Rusty grinned. "Yeah, but think how cool it would be if he could talk back," he said, wiggling his brows and finally squirming away from her.

"Oh yeah," she agreed with a roll of her eyes, mimicking him. "That would be way cool." He sniffled, swiping his nose on his fist. "Come on, brat," Katie said, draping an arm affectionately around his neck. "Let's get you some allergy medicine before you leave for school and then I've got to write a note to your teacher so she can give you your medicine this afternoon."

He came to a dead stop and looked at her in horror. "Ah, Ma, come on," he whined. "You're not going to make me bring a note to the teacher so I can take medicine at school like I'm some wussy girl or some sick weakling, are you?"

At eleven, the most important thing in the world was to avoid at all costs any embarrassment in front of the guys, and taking medicine at school or having your mother write notes to the teacher qualified as definite embarrassments.

"Hey," she said with a laugh, giving him another bump with her hip. "Watch that negative girl talk. I'm a wussy girl, remember?"

He thought about it for a minute, then grinned. "Nah," he said, hip-bumping her in return then dancing away from her. "You're a ma, that's different."

"Yeah, come back and talk to me about wussy girls in about four years, kid." Laughing, Katie swooped, wrapping her arms around him, pulling him close and pasting his face with loud, smacking kisses, her heart flooded with love.

"Stop!" he giggled, trying to squirm away from her. "Ma, stop! Stop kissing me. I'll take my medicine at school," he cried, laughing and breathing hard. "Promise. I promise," he shrieked. Giving him one last, loud, smacking kiss, Katie reluctantly released him.

"Yuck," Rusty complained with a grin, swiping his hand down his cheek.

"Score another for the mother!" Katie said with a triumphant fist pump as she sailed out of the kitchen with her beloved son right behind her to start the first day of their new life.

Chapter Three

The offices of the *Cooper's Cove Carrier* were located right on Main Street, across from the public library and right next door to the only bank in town.

Since the Main Street business section only ran a scant two blocks—right through the heart of town—almost everything was in walking distance to the newspaper offices.

The paper's storefront office boasted one full-time reporter, who was currently on maternity leave, one full-time copy editor, one ad salesman and a part-timer who'd been at the paper since Katie was a child.

Lindsey had started out as an intern while still in high school, and merely stayed, learning and managing the office with the efficiency of a drill sergeant. Katie had no idea what she—or the paper—would do without Lindsey.

While some women got positively giddy over the prospect of an end-of-the-season clothing or shoe sale, for Katie, there was nothing that made her happier than being in a newspaper office.

As a child, she'd spent many happy afternoons at the newspaper, absorbing everything from the reporters transcribing their stories, to the copy editors proofing them, to running the final blue lines—the proofed and copy-edited pages—around the block to the printer on her bicycle.

When her dad was alive, he used to tease that she had newspaper ink running through her veins, not blood. She'd been ten when a heart attack had claimed her dad's life, so the newspaper had passed to his only brother, Cyrus—a lifelong bachelor—who'd given up hope of passing the newspaper on to *his* children.

So it was only natural for Katie's Uncle Cyrus to turn the paper over to her now. They'd agreed to ease in to the transition; he'd work part-time for the first month of her tenure, making certain he was available to answer any and all questions, while she slowly took over all the responsibilities that running a newspaper entailed.

Not wanting to crowd her, her Uncle Cyrus had decided to do his work from his cabin at Cooper's Cove Lake. It would not only give Katie time and space to find her own way, but would also give him an opportunity to take his first real vacation in years.

Katie knew her uncle was only a phone call or a twenty-minute ride away if she needed him, and after practically growing up in the newspaper office, she was pretty well-versed on how everything ran.

On this, her first morning as managing editor, with the warm autumn sun beating down on her, Katie stood just outside the plateglass windows of the newspaper office grinning like a loon.

She'd worked so hard and so long to get here, to belong here, to be qualified and capable of taking over the family newspaper, and now that the day had arrived, she wanted to take just a moment to savor what it had cost her to get here.

It had all been worth it, she thought with a smile. The work and the worry, the long hours and the strained budget, the sacrifices and the tears—because if she hadn't gone through all of *that,* she wouldn't have ended up *here.* And there was nowhere else in the world she'd rather be.

"You're running late," Lindsey blurted before Katie had even gotten through the front door. With her arms full, Katie stopped and stared at the woman.

"Late?" Katie blinked at her. "How can I be late? It's my first day and I just got here."

"I know." With a pen stuck in her hair bun and a steno pad in her hand, Lindsey smiled, shoving her thick glasses up her nose. "But I already set up your appointments for this week and I need to brief you."

Katie laughed. "Lindsey, sometimes your efficiency scares me. But just for this morning, do you think I could get in my office and put my stuff down before you brief me?"

Lindsey glanced at her watch again, then tapped it with a frown. "Well, okay, but you'll have to hurry because you have a luncheon meeting with the mayor and the town council at eleven thirty."

Katie came to an abrupt halt just outside her office door. Again. "I have a luncheon meeting? *Today?*" She already had a million things to do today and lunch hadn't been one of them.

She glanced down at herself, hoping the crisp, pressed jeans and white blouse were suitable for a luncheon meeting. She'd have worn a suit if she'd known about the meeting, but since the movers were coming this afternoon, she decided on comfort over style.

"You look fine," Lindsey assured her with a wave of her hand as if reading Katie's mind, and then she pushed her thick glasses up again.

Resigned, Katie dropped everything in her arms on her already cluttered desk and dug for her day planner, snatching it free from under a pile of edits she needed to go over this morning. If she didn't do this now, she was afraid she'd get too swamped to do it later.

"Okay, Lindsey, before I even get started on this mess, why don't you just bring me up to date?" Katie sank down in the big leather chair behind her desk and opened her day planner.

"First things first," Lindsey said, coming into her office and absently straightening one of the framed newspapers that adorned the wall. "Clarence is out. He said he's going to be gone most of the day, taking orders for ads for the special Halloween issue. I told him not to forget to check in later. Or else," Lindsey said sternly, making Katie grin. Clarence and Lindsey had been going around and around deliberately irritating each other for years.

"We start running the Halloween advertising in two weeks, right?" Katie asked, glancing at her planner and jotting a note to herself about the special Halloween issue. "We're going to need to run a full schedule of the carnival—"

"I'm already on it," Lindsey assured her. "We need to touch base with the police chief to find out about what streets will be closed to traffic during the carnival and make sure we get those printed in next week's issue. I made an appointment for you with the police chief for tomorrow morning so you can give him last year's list of street closings to update and approve." Lindsey didn't allow Katie time to even comment about her meeting with Lucas. "You also need to start thinking about who to interview next for your weekly 'Getting to Know You' column. I think you decided to do this week's column on yourself," Lindsey said with a smile. "But we need to get a couple of columns in the file so that in an emergency, we'll have some back-up. I thought you might want to ask the new chief about an interview since he's new in town as well."

"Good idea," Katie said, making another note. "Do we have a list of who we've done already?"

"The list we've already done is in your bottom file drawer, so take a look at it when you get the chance."

"Will do," Katie said.

"You also need to set up a weekly meeting with the new police chief at a time that's convenient for both of you."

"What for?" Katie demanded, abruptly sitting forward in her chair. She was purposefully trying to avoid Lucas, not make weekly appointments to see him!

"For your 'Police Beat' column," Lindsey said

calmly. "The weekly rundown of all the police activity in town for the previous week, remember?"

"I remember," Katie said glumly, wondering if she could pawn this job off on someone else—then she realized there *was no one else*. She was the boss and this was her responsibility.

Not a problem, she assured herself. If she couldn't avoid Lucas, then she'd simply fall back on her tried-and-true system of treating him like a big brother. It worked with every other man the past six years, surely it would work with him.

She hoped.

"And then you also have to talk to the chief about the special safety article for the Halloween issue. That's an annual feature. I've already pulled last year's column for you. It's in that blue file on your desk, so you can just take it to him and discuss all the updates." Lindsey hesitated a moment. "Oh, and your mother called to tell you something," she said, trying to keep a straight face. Lady Louella's eccentricity was well known in town, but that didn't make her any less adored by nearly everyone. Her mother was just accepted as another character—which the town was full of.

"What?" Katie asked, and Lindsey chuckled.

"Sorry, Katie, but your mom couldn't remember why she called or what she wanted to tell you, but she said if she did remember, she'd call you back."

"Okay," Katie said, shaking her head and chuckling as well. Her mother's short-term memory lapses were part of the damage left by a minor stroke last year. But the doctors were certain eventually her mother's memory would come back. Until then it made life with her mother interesting—if nothing else.

"Oh, one final thing," Lindsey said. "We need to reserve some space for the special election coverage. We may even have to do an additional four-page section."

"So it *is* an election year," Katie said, remembering making that comment to Lucas this morning.

"Oh, yeah," Lindsey said. "And Mayor Hannity is not pleased that there's rumors that this time around he's not going to run unopposed."

"Do you really think anyone will have the guts to run against him? I mean, he's been mayor for almost twenty years."

"There's talk," Lindsey admitted.

"Sounds to me like someone wants to *shed* blood. I don't know that I'd take on Harry Hannity in an election or anything else," Katie admitted with a shake of her head. "I mean the man's practically an institution in town." Katie adored the mayor who had been "keeping company" with her mother since a few years after her father's death.

"Then perhaps you might want to mention that to your mother," Lindsey said carefully. "Since it's your mother who's been threatening to run against him."

Katie stared at her in shock. "You're kidding? You must mean someone else's mother, not *my* mother."

Good grief, her mother couldn't remember something from one hour to the next, how on earth did she think she could run the entire town? And why on earth would she be threatening to run against a man she'd been seeing for almost twenty years? This didn't make sense, Katie realized, but then not a lot her mother did—did.

"Oh, yeah, Katie, it's *your* mother." Lindsey chuckled. "And everyone in town is talking about it. Apparently she's still steamed about Mayor Hannity canceling the seniors' monthly potluck dinner and she's been threatening to run against him ever since."

Katie groaned. "I'll talk to her, Lindsey. I'm sure this is just some kind of misunderstanding. Or she's merely trying to get the mayor's goat." Katie leaned forward. "And I don't want one word printed about my mother possibly running for mayor until I have a chance to talk to her." Talk her out of it was more like it, Katie thought. "No matter what my mother says," she added just to be on the safe side.

Lindsey shrugged. "Hey, it's your paper," she said, and Katie felt a thrill of pride. Yes, she realized, it really finally was.

She glanced at the clock on the wall. "If there's nothing else, I've got to get some work done before I leave for that luncheon." Katie's brows drew together as she reviewed her notes, wondering if there was any part of her job that didn't involve meeting with or seeing the new police chief?

Lucas had no intention of going to the mayor's luncheon today since he was still far too busy trying to get the department organized, but when Mayor Hannity came upstairs from his own office to Lucas's, and offered to walk over to the diner with him, Lucas didn't have much choice but to go.

Now, as Lucas sat at a back table, surrounded by the town council and the mayor, his thoughts drifted back to Katie again. And as if his mind simply conjured her up, she pushed through the front door, looking a little frazzled and more than a little tired, surprising him.

She looked just as beautiful now as she had this morning in her terry cloth robe and bunny slippers. The crisp, white long-sleeved blouse, and the snug-fitting jeans that she had on hugged her curves in a way that almost had him drooling.

Her hair had been pulled up to some kind of knot atop her head, but several strands had sprung free and were now framing that gorgeous face, begging to be touched, stroked and caressed.

Her gaze met his and for an instant it seemed as if time and the world had frozen, until he forced himself to look away, to scold himself and remind himself that he wasn't interested in this woman, in *any* woman. He couldn't afford to be, not anymore.

"I'm sorry I'm late, Mayor," Katie said with a smile, hurrying over to the table and bending to kiss his cheek. "It couldn't be helped." She'd known him since she was a child, and in spite of his political reputation, beneath his blustery exterior he was a sweet, gentle man with a kind heart.

"Hey, Katherine, are we all going to get a kiss hello?" Patrick Flannigan, the fire chief who had seven grown sons and was old enough to be her grandfather, teased with a wink. She pulled out the only empty chair, between the mayor and Lucas, and sat down as everyone chuckled at his joke.

"Hi," Lucas said quietly.

"Hi yourself," she returned, glancing at him. Her stomach immediately tied into knots, as did her tongue, so she tried to simply ignore him.

"Hey, Lucas, heard you had some female trouble at your place last night?" one of the council members called across the table, causing Katie's head to snap up. She almost groaned. Good grief! Obviously the rumor mill was up and running at full speed.

"Yeah, Lucas, Patience said there was some commotion at your place in the middle of the night," another member added, wiggling his brows suggestively. "Heard it involved a mysterious woman."

Patience Pettibone owned the diner and spread gossip faster than other towns spread epidemics.

"Well, you know how it is," Lucas said with a smile and a shrug. "Some women just can't leave a man alone."

Almost choking on the water she'd just sipped, Katie's eyes narrowed on Lucas as her temper began to simmer.

What on earth did he think he was doing?

Surely he wasn't about to tell everyone what had happened last night? He wouldn't dare embarrass her like that, would he? Her water glass slammed down on the table, almost sloshing over the rim.

"Gather it wasn't a planned tryst then," Patrick said with a sly grin of his own.

"No, actually, she kind of took me by surprise," Lucas said, reaching for a roll out of the basket being passed around. "I really wasn't expecting her." Smiling, he passed the basket to Katie and she almost snapped his fingers off as she snatched it from him.

"That's cute, Lucas," she muttered for his ears only. "Real cute. What on earth do you think you're doing?" she hissed, wanting to bean him with the breadbasket.

"I wouldn't mind having a female surprise me in the middle of the night," the mayor grumbled. "Might perk things up a bit around here."

"I guess that all depends on the female," Lucas said, breaking his roll apart. "This one was a real spitfire, I tell you. It took everything I had and then some to handle her." He chuckled. "For a while there, I thought I was going to have to call in reinforcements. And Patrick, you were the first person to come to mind." He grinned, a pure male grin that had Katie's temper going straight to boil. "But I managed to get the job done by myself."

"Lucas!" Katie growled under her breath in warning. He was making it sound as if they'd had some illicit sexual tryst last night!

"I'm not ashamed to tell you she nearly wore me out," Lucas added with a smile and Katie just hung her head, wishing the floor would open up and swallow her.

She was simply going to have to kill him, she decided. Something slow and gruesome. No, on second thought, death was too good for him. She'd think of something worse—something *far* worse. And then she'd just plead insanity. It was the only defense a single mother had.

"But, it all worked out well in the end," Lucas said with a smile. "And we both ended up getting what we wanted," he added with a careless shrug, causing Katie to start choking on the bread she'd been chewing.

Absently, Lucas reached over and patted her back, picking up her water glass and handing it to her, grateful she didn't throw it at him.

"And I've got six beautiful brand new pups to give away this morning as a result if anyone's interested," Lucas added with a smile, glancing around the table at the chorus of laughter.

"Dogs?" Patrick glanced around the table in confusion. "Are you saying the commotion at your house last night in the middle of the night was a female *dog?*"

"Not just a dog, Patrick," Lucas corrected solemnly. "But a pregnant female sheltie. Most beautiful thing you've ever seen. Stop by the house and I'll show you the pups," he offered with a smile, giving Katie a wink as she let out a long, silent sigh of relief.

Okay, so maybe she wouldn't have to kill the blasted man after all.

"They'd make a great addition to the firehouse, Patrick. Keep you company during the down times." The pups had actually been born two nights ago, but Lucas wasn't about to tell anyone that, nor was he going to impeach Katie or her reputation just for the sake of gossip. How word got out that he'd had some kind of commotion involving a woman at his house last night simply amazed him. He had a feeling small town life was going to take some getting used to.

"You know, now that might not be a bad idea," the fire chief muttered, stroking his chin in thought. "Not a bad idea at all."

"Well, if we're done talking about women, I'd like to get down to business," the mayor announced.

"Good idea," Lucas said, reaching for Katie's hand under the table and giving it a reassuring squeeze.

"Ma," Rusty yelled from his bedroom, his voice echoing down the long hall. "How much longer do I gotta do this?"

"Until it's done," Katie called back, climbing over several boxes as she searched for a lamp. It was after six, she was exhausted. It would be dark soon and she didn't want to be searching around in the dark for a light.

The movers had left about two hours ago, leaving boxes piled everywhere. Furniture had been set up in their proper rooms, but they still had to unpack.

Hopping down off a box with a frown, Katie scanned the living room/dining room combination, trying to remember which box had lamps in it.

Maybe if she wasn't so excited she could think better. Shaking her head, she pushed her hair off her face, trying to concentrate. This house—*her* house—had been a dream for so long, that tonight, actually knowing that dream had become a reality seemed almost surreal.

She had to keep walking through the rooms—actually, stepping onto boxes was more like it—just to see everything, to remind herself this was *hers. And Rusty's.*

It wasn't a new house by any means, but it was a comfortable one, large enough for Rusty to have his own bedroom, and for her to have a rather spacious master bedroom with her own bathroom. As a bonus, there was also an extra bedroom down the hall for her office.

At the back of the house was a huge, sprawling family room adjacent to the kitchen, complete with a fire-place for frosty winter evenings.

Although the house needed updating, Katie wasn't in a hurry. When she looked around, she didn't see what was there, but what *could be—would be* once she got through with it. The possibilities were enough to make her giddy.

Glancing around at the trail of boxes leading every-where, Katie grinned again, then scolded herself for stalling. She had to find those lamps and get a path cleared and some of this stuff put away before morning.

And then of course, she thought with a weary sigh, she had to think about dinner.

Moving a box with her foot, she grinned in triumph, opening it to find her living room lamps neatly tucked into it. She pulled them out, set them on a couple of boxes on either side of the living room, turned them on and went back to work.

"How you doing, honey?" she called, about thirty minutes later, wondering why it was so quiet in Rusty's bedroom.

"Fine, Ma." His voice was muffled and so dejectedly put-upon she had to smile. He'd been in his room, try-ing to unpack his boxes and set up his room since he'd come home from Sean's.

"We'll work just until it's full dark, honey," she called, "and then how about if we get a pizza?"

"With sausage?"

She laughed. "With anything you want," she prom-ised, opening another box. "We just need to get our bed-rooms in some order so we can sleep, and I need to get a few more boxes unpacked so we can at least move around a bit."

The doorbell rang and Katie frowned, wondering who on earth was at the door. Probably just a neighbor. Or her mother and aunt, she thought, wondering if her mother had ever remembered what she wanted to tell her. Her mom had called the office two more times today, but unfortunately she still couldn't recall what she wanted to tell Katie.

Pushing her hair back again, Katie carefully threaded her way over the stacks of boxes to the front door.

She paused for a moment and glanced down at herself, then groaned. Some impression she was going to make if it was a new neighbor. She'd had on her oldest, paint-stained jeans that were a few sizes too small now and worn white nearly everywhere. The sweatshirt she wore had lost its sleeves somewhere and was also full of paint—unfortunately it didn't match the colors on her jeans.

She'd yanked her hair back into a ponytail, but that had been hours ago, and now, strands were loose and drooping around her face.

When the doorbell pealed again, Katie forgot her appearance and yanked open the front door. Her mouth dropped open, almost hitting her tennis shoes.

"Lucas?"

Before he had a chance to respond, Rusty's scream of fear shattered the silence. "Ma! Help. Get it off me! Ma, hurry!" Before she could even move, Lucas was gently nudging her aside.

"Where is he?"

"Down the hall. Third door on the right," she said, pointing as Rusty screamed again.

"Rusty? I'm coming, honey." She tried to follow Lucas, hurrying behind him, but his legs were much longer and he'd traversed the line of boxes in a few short steps, racing down the hallway toward her son's bedroom.

With her heart beating a percussion rhythm, she hopped over the last of the boxes, and headed down the hall at a run. She pushed open Rusty's door just in time to see Lucas sitting on the floor, cradling her prone son.

"You're okay now, son," Lucas soothed, glancing down at the boy as he held him close. "You're okay."

"Rusty?" Terrified, Katie went to her son and knelt down beside him, running her hands over his arms and legs, wanting to assure herself he was all right. "What happened?" She glanced around, saw his box spring and mattress were not where they were the last time she was in his room.

"He tried to move his bed," Lucas said. "He couldn't quite manage it and the box spring came down on top of him." Lucas glanced down at Rusty. "But he held his own for awhile there," he said, not wanting to embarrass the boy further.

"Hey, mister?" Confusion glistened in Rusty's green eyes. "Uh…who are you?"

Lucas laughed, his gaze meeting Katie's over Rusty's head.

"I'm sorry," she said with a shake of her head. "Honey, this is Lucas Porter, the chief of police."

"Police?" Rusty said, his eyes darting from his mom

to Lucas then back again. "You're a cop?" He craned his neck around Lucas to see his mother. "Am I in trouble or something, Ma?"

Laughing, Lucas slowly stood, righting the boy as he did, making certain Rusty's legs were steady before he released him. "No, son, you're not in any trouble."

"Then how come you're here? I thought cops only came if there was trouble," Rusty said.

"I'm not here because I'm a cop or the chief of police," Lucas explained. "Actually, I'm here looking for…" He pulled a piece of paper out of his back pocket and glanced at it. "I'm looking for Jed Jackson Murphy," Lucas said, glancing at Rusty again.

"That's me," Rusty said. "I'm Jed Jackson Murphy. But everyone calls me Rusty." Wide-eyed, he stared up at Lucas and swiped at his nose as he frowned. "So why you looking for me if I'm not in trouble?"

With a smile, Lucas folded the piece of paper slowly, putting it back into his pocket. "Well, son, it seems that I'm your buddy."

"Huh?"

"You?" Katie said, trying to hide her shock. "You're Rusty's *buddy?*" She shook her head. "Wait, I don't understand. I didn't sign Rusty up for a…" Her voice trailed off. "Mother," she said, nodding her head in understanding. "Now I know what she kept forgetting to tell me." Her mother must have signed Rusty up for the Buddy for a Boy program and that's what she kept forgetting to tell Katie. "You're Rusty's buddy? *Really?*" She wasn't quite sure she believed this, it was as if her mother and the Gods were conspiring against her, doing

everything in their power to throw her and this man together.

"Afraid so," Lucas said with a sheepish grin, slipping
his hands in his pockets as she sagged against the bedroom wall.

"Uh…Ma?" Rusty looked at Katie nervously.
"Sean's my buddy," he clarified with a confused scowl.
"I know Sean. We been buddies forever." Her jerked a
thumb at Lucas. "I don't know this guy, so how can he
be my buddy?"

Chuckling, Katie ruffled her son's hair, frowning
when he winced. "Rusty, Lucas isn't that kind of
buddy," she absently explained, slowly running her fingers over his scalp to search for any signs of injury as
she talked. "A Buddy is a special program in Cooper's
Cove."

"May I?" Lucas asked with a lift of his brow.

"Be my guest," she said, extending her other hand to
encourage Lucas to go ahead. She couldn't wait to see
how he handled this. And her son.

"Rusty, my name is Lucas Porter, and I am the chief
of police. But I'm also what's called a Buddy." He
smiled at the suspicion in the boy's eyes. "What that
means is, we have a special program in town, one that
lets boys who don't have fathers…sort of borrow…fa-
thers, but they're not really fathers, they're friends.
Friends who don't have any children. So, we take a boy
with no father and a father without a child, and we
match them together so they can learn from one another
and teach one another. And be buddies."

"You mean buddies like Sean's my buddy?"

"That's right," Lucas confirmed. "You and I will be buddies just like you and Sean."

"Yeah, 'cepting you're bigger." Rusty tilted his head back. "Much bigger."

"That's right. But I don't just get to be a buddy to you. You get to be a buddy to me."

"I get to be *your* buddy? So what do I gotta do?"

Lucas shrugged. "Nothing really. Nothing more than friends would do. *Men* friends," Lucas said pointedly. "We can watch some games together, play some ball, shoot some hoops, maybe take in a game. Do whatever you like."

"A real live game?" Rusty asked, his voice lilting up in excitement.

"Yep, a real live game." Smiling slowly, Lucas realized it was time to pull out the big guns. "I used to work security for the Chicago Bears during college. I get tickets every year, go into the locker room, talk to the players. So I thought since the season just started, maybe you'd like to take in a Bears game some Sunday?"

The boy's mouth fell open as his eyes widened. "The Chicago Bears," he repeated in whispered awe. "You're gonna take me to see a real live Bears game?" Shaking his head in disbelief, Rusty grinned. "Awesome."

Grateful he'd scored some points, Lucas smiled. "There's some things I know how to do that I'll be happy to share with you and show you. If you'll show me and share with me some of things you know and like to do. Isn't that what buddies do?"

"I guess." Rusty paused, then grinned suddenly. "I

can spit almost seven feet," he crowed proudly, pushing his tongue between the space between his two front teeth, ready to demonstrate.

"Rusty!" Katie's breath hissed out as Lucas's lips twitched.

"That's quite impressive." Lucas rocked back on his heels, tucking his tongue in his cheek. "But I held the third-grade record." His grin was full of masculine pride. "Seven feet, six inches."

"Sweet," Rusty said with a grin of his own, impressed. "So what else can you do?"

Lucas was thoughtful. "Well, let's see. I thought maybe we could build a clubhouse—"

"A real clubhouse? Just for guys? No wussy sissy girls allowed?" Rusty said, glancing at his mother.

"Hey, watch it," Katie cautioned with a smile. Watching her son, seeing the excitement shimmering in his eyes at the prospect of doing things—male things—with an adult male made her heart ache for all that her son had missed by losing his own dad so early. And made her wonder how on earth Lucas could have such an easy, instinctive rapport with a child when he apparently didn't have any.

"Definitely just for guys," Lucas said, ignoring Katie and giving her son all his attention.

"With steps and a floor and everything?" Excitement had Rusty all but dancing in place again.

"Steps and everything," Lucas confirmed, straightening.

"So what else can you do, huh? Can you play baseball?"

"Starting pitcher in high school."

"Can you play football?"

"Quarterback. Varsity team, junior and senior year."

Rusty whistled, impressed. "What else?"

"Well, instead of just telling you, how about I show you?" Lucas asked, watching delight glisten in the boy's eyes as his feet danced in excitement.

"Show me? Now? Like right now?" Rusty asked, nearly bouncing out of his tennis shoes.

"Rusty," Katie cautioned, glancing around the room. It was pitch-black outside and a mess inside. "Right now isn't exactly what I'd call a good time."

"Your mom's right, son. How about if I help you unpack some of this stuff and get your room set up?" Lucas smiled. "Then tomorrow after school we can talk some more if it's all right with your mom?" Lucas shrugged, glancing at Katie for approval. He waited for her nod before continuing. "Then this weekend I thought maybe we could drive up to Cooper's Cove Lake and do some fishing."

"With real live bait?" Motioning Lucas down so he could whisper, Rusty gave his mom a weak smile. "My mom hates worms," he whispered to Lucas. "So I ain't never used night crawlers."

"Nor proper English," Katie said mildly to no one in particular.

Nodding in understanding, Lucas straightened. "Well, I know this bait shop right near the lake that sells only fresh night crawlers. I've got some poles and a couple of tackle boxes filled with fishing gear, so if we can maybe talk your mom into making us some sandwiches we can have a real picnic." He glanced at Katie. "And some weekend if you and your friends want to have a campout or a sleepover at the lake—with your mom's permission of course—we can arrange that as well." He smiled at the boy, who was staring at him, nearly slack jawed. "I own a cabin up at the lake," he said by way of explanation.

Rusty's grin, quick and bright, warmed Katie's heart. "Can I tell Sean and the guys?"

Letting out a breath he didn't know he'd been holding, Lucas smiled, ruffling Rusty's curly hair. "You can tell anyone you like."

"Awesome," Rusty said, then frowned, rubbing his empty stomach. "Ma, when can we get our pizza? I'm starving," he added with a groan.

"I tell you what," Lucas said before Katie had a chance to open her mouth. "Let's get your room pulled together and then I'll take you and your mom out for a pizza."

"Really?" Rusty cocked his head. "With sausage and cheese and stuff?" His brows furrowed. "But no 'shrooms or spinach. Weeds and fungus. Yuck." Holding his stomach, he made a barfing sound that had Katie rolling her eyes and Lucas chuckling.

"My sentiments exactly," Lucas said, his gaze meeting Katie's. He ignored the hot rush of desire that coiled inside of him, pushing it aside to concentrate only on the boy.

The kid was the spitting image of his mother both in looks and personality. Definitely a spitfire with a zest and curiosity for life that was infectious.

Feeling better than he had in a good, long time, Lucas held out his hand. It was the first lesson he'd learned from his own father and had taught to his son. When a man gave his word, he shook on it, and kept it. "So, do we have a deal?"

Grinning, Rusty wiped his hand down his jeans, then solemnly took Lucas's hand and shook it, puffing out his chest at being treated like a *man*. "Deal. Buddies?"

"Buddies," Lucas confirmed with a nod.

Watching them, Katie nervously rubbed her own hands together. "Uh, Lucas, are you sure about this? It's not necessary, really." She wasn't quite sure why the man unnerved her so, but his presence was so powerful, so masculine, it made her feel as if her lungs had somehow come up short of oxygen.

She glanced at Rusty, saw the joy on his face, the excited anticipation, and knew she hadn't seen such joy in his face in a long, long time. It warmed her heart and made it ache for all that she couldn't give to her son.

Her son needed this, she realized with a pang. Needed the presence and influence of a man perhaps more than she'd ever realized. And regardless of how nervous Lucas made her feel, or how she felt or didn't feel about him, she had to do whatever was in her power to give this precious gift to her son.

"It is necessary," Lucas corrected with a smile, taking her by the shoulders and turning her around to show her the door. A quick flash of need and desire swept through her from his touch, scaring her. "Really. Now give us about…" He glanced back at Rusty for confirmation. "An hour?" he asked with a lift of his brow and

Rusty nodded. "I promise by then we'll have the room set up, and some of these boxes unpacked and put away, and then we'll go for pizza."

"But—"

"Go," Lucas said softly, his hands still warming her shoulders, his voice soft and gentle as it fluttered against her ear, making her entire body shiver. "This is called the bonding part," he whispered in her ear. "A chance for us to get to know one another, without mom."

She wasn't certain she liked the "without mom" part, but she realized with a sigh that Rusty was growing up and did need the calm, stable influence of a man—a man who could teach him all the things a father would have, all the things a boy needed to grow up to be a good person, a good man, a good father and husband.

"All right," she said with a nod and started toward the door. "An hour," she repeated numbly.

Shaking her head, Katie scrubbed her hands over her face, trying to make sense of all of this. Well, she conceded, heading back into the living room to tackle some more boxes, she wanted Rusty to have this, she wanted her son to have everything good in the world he needed to grow up to be a good person. And if that meant having Lucas Porter in his life, well, she was simply going to have to accept it, and curtail her own emotions and feelings for her son's sake.

Opening one of the boxes and staring blindly at the contents, she realized that, as for her own wayward feelings about Lucas, she'd just revert back to Plan B.

She'd treat him like a big brother. She couldn't go wrong with that. Unfortunately what Lucas made her feel didn't seem very brotherly, Katie thought and closed her eyes on a sigh. But for her sake and her son's sake that's all Lucas could ever be.

Realizing this, Katie felt a deep yearning in her heart, a yearning she hadn't quite been so aware of until she ran into Lucas Porter.

But she just had to pack that yearning away in the same place she'd packed away all her youthful dreams, along with the one about having children and a wonderful, loving partner and husband, and of course the happily-ever-after.

She'd had it, for a little while, she recalled sadly. But those weren't the cards she'd subsequently been dealt. What she'd been dealt was a life where the responsibilities of protecting her son and her mother came first. And as for the rest, well, she had to be grateful for all that she had, since it was so much more than most.

But still, she thought as she leaned against the living room wall, maybe it wouldn't hurt to just daydream a little bit about Lucas, and what never could be.

Chapter Four

"I'm done, Ma," Rusty said, shoving away his plate with a half a piece of pizza still left. "I'm stuffed." He rubbed his stomach and grinned. "Can I go play some of the video games now?"

Katie glanced at her watch, then at the noisy crowd in the pizza parlor. Every booth and table was full, and there was a line at the counter, and behind almost every video game in the place.

Apparently they weren't the only ones celebrating the first day of school with a pizza.

"Rusty, I don't know. It's a school night and—"

"Ma, come on," Rusty wheedled, fidgeting in the booth next to her. "It's early yet, and my room's all done, right, Lucas?" Grinning, Rusty looked across the booth at him for support.

"Yeah," Lucas said slowly. "It is," he admitted sheepishly. "We finished his entire room before we left, Katie, dressers and all." He shrugged his apology, not wanting to appear as if he was taking sides.

"And I don't got any homework, so all I gotta do is fall into bed when I get home. Come on, Ma, please? Only fifteen minutes. Please? Please?"

Laughing, Katie reached in her purse to get some money from her wallet. Lucas had already insisted on paying the pizza bill and leaving the tip. "Okay, fifteen minutes and then it's straight home, and a shower," she added, causing Rusty to make a face. "And then to bed," she corrected, handing him the bill for the video games.

"Awesome." He bounded out of the booth before she had a chance to change her mind, leaving her and Lucas alone.

There was an awkward moment of silence, and then Katie relaxed, telling herself she was being ridiculous. She probably shouldn't have come since this should have been Lucas's time with Rusty, but it was hard to regret it when she'd been having such a lovely time.

This wasn't a date; Lucas wasn't interested in *her*, she reminded herself firmly. And there was nothing, absolutely nothing wrong with enjoying herself with her son's buddy.

Lucas was here—they were both here—because of her son and their mutual concern about his welfare, so nothing about this evening should make her feel uncomfortable or guilty.

"This was very nice of you, Lucas," Katie said, feeling just a little self-conscious and tongue-tied now that they were alone. Or at least alone in the booth surrounded by probably half the town.

Lucas chuckled. "Hey, I've got to eat, too. But I have to admit, when I left the house this evening I never anticipated, never thought that I'd be spending the evening with you." Realizing what he said, Lucas took a sip of his soda, wondering why being around this woman made him feel like a sixteen-year-old with his foot in his mouth. And his hormones on overdrive.

She laughed. "Well, I don't know who was more surprised when I opened the front door. You or me." She shook her head. "My mother's been calling me all day to tell me something. But she simply couldn't remember what it was. I think she kept calling to tell me she signed Rusty up for the Buddy for a Boy program, but every time she called, she couldn't remember what she wanted to tell me."

"Ahh," Lucas said with a nod. "So you really didn't know anything about it."

"Not a thing," Katie admitted with a smile. "Although you mentioned it this morning when you were at the house, it didn't occur to me that my mother would have signed Rusty up." She shrugged. "But I'm glad she did." Her gaze searched the crowd for her son. She spotted him, then relaxed. "I think it will be good for Rusty."

"I do, too," Lucas said, following the train of her gaze to Rusty.

"Lucas?"

He turned his head and met her eyes. "Yes?"

"Tell me something," she said, propping her elbows on the table and her chin on her hands. "I can understand why my mom signed up Rusty for this program, but why did you sign up?" She chuckled. "I mean, I'm sure you have tons more important things to do than spend your free time with a boy you don't even know."

She was trying not to be touched by the fact that he'd done just that, had agreed to so freely give of himself and his time to a fatherless boy. It was an incredibly unselfish thing to do and told her a lot about the man.

"Why not?" He shrugged, feeling a sliver of alarm at the personal bent the conversation had suddenly taken. He couldn't ever tell her that the loss of his son— missing his boy every single day—was like a giant, empty hole inside of him that nothing, absolutely nothing, seemed to fill.

He'd thought long and hard and very seriously before he'd even considered volunteering for the Buddy for a Boy program, then realized that perhaps, just perhaps it might do him and his aching heart some good.

He loved children, *adored* them, and had always wanted a big family just like he'd grown up in. Unfortunately, his wife had refused to even consider more children as long as he was a cop.

Now, after everything that had happened, he didn't know if he should be relieved or grateful.

And Rusty was such a pistol of a kid loaded with boundless optimism, curiosity and energy, Lucas was certain spending time with the boy would be just the soothing balm his ailing heart needed.

He looked at Katie as he continued to try to explain. "As the new police chief, the mayor thinks it's important for me to get involved in the community. And so do I. I must admit I've never lived in a small town before. Amos Mayfield had been a fixture as police chief for years, and I know sometimes change is hard for people to accept. I thought it was important to become as involved in the community as possible so that folks get to know me, and accept me which is why I've volunteered for several of the town's programs, not just the Buddy program." He glanced around the pizza parlor, returning the wave of Artie Roberts, the mechanic at the town's garage. He really was beginning to like the small town feel of Cooper's Cove, getting to know everyone, knowing everyone knew him. It was quite a change from the big city of Chicago where he was lucky if he knew his next door neighbor.

"Sounds reasonable," Katie admitted with a smile. "So I take it you don't have any children of your own?"

"No." The answer was clipped and flat, making Katie's eyes widen. Uh-oh. She'd stepped into something—what, she wasn't sure, but his voice and face had changed and she could feel the chill all the way across the booth.

Clearly, she'd crossed into the realm of his personal life and apparently Lucas wasn't keen on talking to her about his personal life. Was it because she was a woman? she wondered. Or because she was a reporter?

At the moment, she wasn't certain. But one thing she did know was that it was rare for a man to have such an innate ability with children when he didn't have any of his own. Her curiosity as a mother and a reporter were aroused.

"Well, I think it's wonderful of you to donate your

time to kids who wouldn't otherwise have an opportunity to do things with an adult male."

"It can't be easy being a single parent," he said softly, and Katie smiled.

"I don't think it's ever easy being a parent," she admitted. "Single or otherwise. But yeah, being a single mom does present some additional problems." She met his intense gaze, then had to wipe her damp hands down her jeans, wishing her heart wasn't beating so fast. "Sometimes it's hard being the one who always has to make and enforce the rules," she admitted with a sigh. "And sometimes it would be nice to just have someone else, another adult to bounce things off of, and sometimes it would be nice to just have twenty-four hours off." Her gaze found her son again and she was flooded with love. "But no matter how rough it gets, how tired I get, or how much I hate being the bad guy, Rusty makes it all worth it. He's an incredible kid and I wouldn't have it any other way."

"Yeah, he is an incredible kid, Katie," Lucas agreed softly, touched by the depth of her feelings for her child and the way she seemingly juggled all the responsibilities she had to make sure she gave everyone their due. Absently, he reached across the table and covered her hand with his. He'd been itching to touch her from the moment she'd opened the door to him tonight. "And you're doing a fabulous job with him."

She chuckled, but didn't remove her hand. His touch was warm, and comforting, and just for a moment she was going to allow herself to enjoy it. Maybe it was just because she was so tired, and her defenses were down.

It had been an incredibly hectic day, exciting but hectic, and she was exhausted. "Thanks. That's always nice to hear."

"Well, well, well, what have we here?" Patience Pettibone stood next to their booth, a wide grin of mischief on her ruby lips.

Katie glanced up with a weak smile and almost groaned. She had to admit, she adored Patience—even if she was Cooper's Cove's version of the town crier.

Sweet, giggly, and totally immune to what others thought about her, Patience had more natural confidence than any woman Katie had ever met. Her complexion was the color of cloves and her eyes were a deeper, dancing brown. Her silver Brillo pad of hair was buzz cut to better decorate the top of her head, with temporary hair dye reflecting whatever holiday was in season.

"Patience," Katie said, managing at the last minute not to groan the woman's name when she realized Lucas was still covering her hand with his. And Patience was all but hovering over their booth, taking everything in. "Nice to see you. You know Lucas Porter, the new police chief, don't you?"

"My, my, my, I surely do," Patience said, giving her colorful hair a pat. "I'm not so old, sugar, that I'd let such a fine, handsome specimen of a man get by me." She batted her fake eyelashes at Lucas. "Evening, chief. Now tell me, what brings you and Katie together this fine fall evening?"

"Business," Katie gasped out before Lucas could open his mouth. "Strictly business," Katie assured the woman with a weak smile. She was such a terrible liar. Patience was going to call her on it any minute, she was sure of it. And then tell her mother she'd caught Katie lying.

Good Lord, that was the last thing she wanted, second only to Patience gossiping about her and Lucas, and telling the whole town they were holding hands at the pizza parlor.

Patience's brows moved up and down like nervous little worms. "Business, huh?"

She chuckled loudly, causing almost everyone in the pizza parlor to turn in their direction. Katie wanted to crawl under the table.

"What kind of business requires hand-holding?" Patience winked at Lucas as her gaze zeroed in on their linked hands. "Monkey business, I think. Yes, siree, monkey business." She chuckled. "Looks like we got ourselves a budding romance here."

"No, actually, Patience," Lucas said calmly, "this really *is* business," he said. "Yes, see, I'm Katie's son's buddy." He smiled. "You know, the Buddy for a Boy program the town council recently started?"

"Yeah," Patience replied, cocking her head a bit. "So what's that got to do with hand-holding?"

Lucas's smile remained firmly in place. "Well, Katie and I aren't exactly holding hands," he clarified, giving Patience his most sincere smile. "We're actually just having a friendly argument that maybe you can help us solve."

"Argument?" Katie repeated weakly, wondering what Lucas was up to this time. Then she remembered the way he'd handled the gossip in the diner at lunch this morning and tried to relax a bit.

"Yes, Katie," Lucas said with a reassuring smile. "Patience strikes me as a modern woman, let's see what she has to say about this. I think she can help us settle this once and for all."

Patience grinned. "You want my help. Well, it's about dang time someone in this town appreciates me. Now, push over, Chief," Patience said, getting into their booth and bumping Lucas's hip with her own ample one as she squeezed in beside him. "If I'm going to be helping you and settling things, then I need to rest my old, weary bones." Chuckling again, she patted her hair. "I think better when I'm sitting, anyway." She smoothed down her black top. "Okay, now what's the problem, here?"

"Well, Patience," Lucas began, still covering Katie's hand, "I say since I invited Rusty for a get-aquatinted pizza, and of course I invited his mom so Rusty wouldn't feel awkward—"

"'Course, that's understandable," Patience said with a bob of her head. "Boys that age feel awkward 'bout just about everything," she said, leaning across the table as if speaking only to Katie. "Nothing strange about that."

"Well, now I say it's only polite to let me pay and leave the tip since I did the inviting." Lucas turned toward Katie again and flashed her a wink. "But Katie here is insisting that I let her pay her share." He lifted their linked hands, and showed Patience the tip money he'd laid down on the table before she'd arrived. "See, she's trying to push this money off on me, to pay for her share. And I say since I did the inviting, I should pay. Now, as a modern woman, what do you think?"

"Sugar, have you gone daft?" Patience demanded of Katie. "When a handsome man offers to buy you a meal, you accept, sugar. You don't argue with him."

"But…but…"

"But nothing, sugar, take it from me," Patience said with a sharp wave of a bejeweled finger. "You may be a modern woman and all, but Katie, you've got to let a man be a *man*." She wiggled her brows knowingly. "Know what I mean? And trust me, girl, you're not getting any younger and if a handsome, available man like the chief here offers to buy you a pizza, even if it's just so he can get to know your boy, you accept and be done with it." Patience shrugged her shoulders. "Who knows, maybe someday he might even show some interest in you. I mean I doubt it since you're such a skinny little thing, and men like a woman that's got some solid meat on her bones." Grinning, she ran a hand down her ample figure. "Like me. But like I said, sugar, you surely ain't getting any younger. And a woman could do a lot worse. Trust me, that comes from experience," Patience added with another chuckle that had her slapping the table at her own humor. "Now, you just stop being so blasted stubborn, Katherine." She drew back, her eyebrows drawing together again. "Why, what would your mama say if she knew you were being downright rude to the new police chief, after he'd been so nice to your boy?"

"But I…I…"

"I know what you're gonna say, sugar," Patience snapped, waving away whatever protest she thought Katie was going to make. "You're gonna say you don't want him thinking or getting the wrong idea. Hell, he's

a man, sugar, let him think or get any idea he wants."
She winked. "The day a mere man can outthink us
hasn't come down the pike yet." Patting her head again,
she stood up, planted her hands on her hips and looked
from one to the other. "Now, are we settled here?" Patience knocked a bejeweled fist to the table to get
Katie's attention. "Really, Katherine, I wouldn't want
to have to tell your mama you were being rude
now—"

"No. No of course not," Katie said with a shake of
her head and a weak smile. She looked at Lucas, saw
the mischief dancing in his eyes and had to hang onto
her laughter. "And you're right, Patience," she said solemnly. "I'll apologize."

"See that you do, sugar. Now, is there anything else?"
Her sharp gaze went from Katie to Lucas and back
again as Katie and Lucas looked at one another, twin
grins trying to sneak free.

"Well, Patience, just one more thing. Are you going
to be in the diner tomorrow?" Lucas asked, making
Katie frown and wonder what he was up to now.

Patience snorted out a laugh. "Every day of my life,
sugar. Some say the diner is my life."

"I know," Lucas said with a smile. "But you've been
so helpful, I was wondering if you'd mind if I dropped
off a little thank-you gift?"

"Thank-you gift?" Patience beamed. "My, my, my,
my, my, chief, that's hardly necessary, but more than
welcome." She batted her eyelashes at him again. "And
I'll look forward to my present and to seeing you again."

"Good. I'll stop in sometime tomorrow."

"And you know, chief, you got any problems, any problems at all, I'm always happy to help out." Patience leaned down to speak directly into Lucas's ear. "Don't take it too personally, chief, but I just don't think Katie's all that interested in you. Sorry." She gave him a whack on his shoulder that could have felled an oak. "But I'm always available. And you can buy me a pizza or anything else, anytime," she finished with another wiggle of her brows. "Anytime at all, sugar."

"Uh…I'll keep that in mind, Patience," Lucas said with a nod.

"Do that. And I'll see you tomorrow." Patience spotted the mayor across the room and waved her hand in the air. "Yoo-hoo, Mayor, there's something we need to talk about." Patience moved across the pizza parlor, then came to an abrupt halt and turned back toward Katie. "By the way, Katherine, what's this I'm hearing about your mama running for mayor?"

"It's not true," Katie assured her hurriedly. "Mama made a joke about it and someone took it seriously, but it's not true." Katie smiled and held up her hand. "Honest." She hoped.

Patience nodded. "Well then, as long as you're sure…"

"Oh, I am, Patience," Katie said, realizing she was going to have to have that talk with her mother sooner rather than later.

"Okay, then, I'll make sure everyone knows it's not true." Patience nodded and headed off to the mayor's table to harass him.

The moment she was gone, both Katie and Lucas burst out laughing.

"That's the second time today you've managed to save my reputation," Katie said with a grin. "But you realize that by morning everyone in town will think that I was downright rude to the new police chief." Katie rolled her eyes. "No doubt we'll both be getting phone calls from my mother. Yours to apologize for her rude daughter, and mine to tell me she taught me better manners than to be rude to anyone in front of the whole town."

Lucas chuckled and shook his head. "Hey, better that than have them talking about us having a romance."

"True," Katie said with another laugh. "Absolutely true."

"I'm a firm believer in keeping your private life private," Lucas said, watching Patience to make sure she didn't round back on them.

Katie looked at Lucas curiously. "And what's this about a thank-you present?"

Now Lucas grinned and leaned across the table so he wouldn't be overheard. "I've got to get rid of that litter of puppies some way, don't I?"

Katie laughed, but she couldn't think of anyone better than Patience to mother a newborn, motherless puppy. "I think that's a great idea," Katie said. She watched Patience scoot into the mayor's booth. "She's gone on to greener pastures, so maybe we'd better make a run for it," Katie suggested, and Lucas nodded.

"Let's." He pushed out of the booth, keeping a watchful eye on Patience. "Why don't you grab Rusty and I'll meet you both outside? That way no one can say we left together."

"Good idea." With a smile, Katie went to find her son, realizing that for the first time in a long time she'd honestly been having fun.

"It's a beautiful night," Katie said with a contented sigh as she walked next to Lucas. Even though it was early September, the temperature was still in the mid sixties with a slight breeze. The leaves were just beginning to change colors, perfuming everything with the distinctive scent of fall.

Rusty didn't want to be seen walking home with his mother, so he'd darted on ahead, but was still in Kate's sight.

Katie took a deep breath and glanced around the familiar town that she loved so much.

"Can you smell the leaves?" she asked with a contented sigh. It was one of her favorite memories from childhood.

Lucas sniffed the air. "Yeah, that's one of the things I loved most about living in the cabin on the lake, the smells of the seasons."

She turned to look at him, silhouetted by the moon and the old-fashioned gas streetlamps. He had such an incredible face—handsome, and yet so full of character. "That's right, you said you had a cabin at the lake. Is that where you grew up?" she asked carefully, wondering if she was somehow stepping onto dangerous ground again.

He shook his head. "No, I grew up in Chicago," he said surprising her. "Born and raised there. My father was a Chicago police officer for his entire career, but my family has owned a cabin on Cooper's Cove Lake for as long as I can remember, and every summer right after school ended, my dad would load us all up—"

"Us?"

He smiled, bumped his hand against hers as they walked and then absently reached for it, holding her hand in his. He liked the way her hand fit in his, liked the way her touch warmed him. "I have four brothers," he said, laughing at the look of horror that crossed her face. "Yeah, I know, scary, isn't it?"

Katie couldn't help but smile up at Lucas. She could hear the love in his voice, see it on his face when he talked of his family. She understood that kind of deep, committed love toward family since it had always been such a vital and necessary part of her life. She couldn't help but feel attracted by Lucas's devotion to his own family.

Chuckling, Katie shook her head. "Your poor mother. Raising one boy has practically given me gray hairs, I can't imagine raising five." She shuddered. "That would definitely give me gray hairs *and* nightmares."

"I'm sure my mother had a few of her own, considering some of our antics. She'd stay up at the cabin all summer alone with us. My dad would come up every weekend and during his vacation, but most of the time it was just Mom and us boys." Lucas laughed suddenly. "Not that we didn't give her some moments, but she had a firm hand and a calm personality, and we knew just how far we could push her."

"It sounds like you were a close family."

"We were," he admitted, realizing it had been a long time since he'd talked about his parents or brothers. Or anything else about his personal life. "We lost both my parents a few years back."

"I'm so sorry," Katie said, giving his hand a squeeze of comfort as they turned down the quiet street where her house was.

"My dad retired from the force, and planned to move up to the cabin, but then my mom got sick. Cancer. She was gone less than a year later, and then a heart attack took my father less than a year after that." Lucas glanced down at Katie. "They'd been married for over fifty years and my brothers and I figured he just didn't want to go on without her."

"That's really a wonderful story. Sad," she corrected, glancing up just as he glanced down. For a moment, they both froze, their gazes locked. She licked her lips, aware his gaze followed her tongue and sent a chill racing over her. "It's hard to imagine a love that lasts an entire lifetime like that." She didn't care for the wistfulness in her voice. She was just tired, she told herself. "What about your brothers? Where are they?"

Lucas sighed contentedly. "Well, my eldest brother, Peter, is a Chicago cop, as are my two youngest brothers, Jack and Jake—they're twins," he said, grinning down at her. "I'm police chief here, and my other brother, Brian, is actually running for political office in a small suburb of Chicago. Mayor," he said with a shake of his head. "Hard to believe Brian's responsible enough to be running for office." He chuckled. "Brian was the worst of us. A pure hellion who gave my mother more fits than the rest of us combined. And from what I understand he's in one very close race with a woman he's been lusting after for months."

"Oh, the poor man," Katie said with a laugh as they reached the wonderful old-fashioned wraparound front porch of her house. It was one of the reasons she'd bought the house. She'd loved the porch. "I'm sure that just makes it harder on him, knowing his competition is also someone he's interested in."

"I'm going in, Ma," Rusty called as he bolted up the front stairs two at a time. The front door was unlocked, as always, since no one in town ever locked their doors.

"Rusty." The tone of Katie's voice stopped him cold. "Don't you have something to say to Lucas?" she prodded and Rusty grinned sheepishly, whipping around and bolting halfway back down the stairs.

"Oh. Yeah." He lifted his hand in a halfhearted wave. "Thanks, Lucas. For the pizza and stuff." He shuffled his feet, and glanced down, clearly uncomfortable and not certain exactly what to say.

"You're welcome, Rusty. If you're not busy tomorrow, how about if I stop by after school and we can draw up some plans for that clubhouse?"

Even in the dark Katie saw her son's eyes brighten like beacons. "Really?" Rusty began to bounce up and down on his tennis shoes. "Tomorrow? We can do it tomorrow?"

"After your chores and your homework," Katie reminded him with a smile.

"Awright, awright," Rusty complained, then his head lifted again. "How 'bout you come over around four,

Lucas? I get home at three and that will give me a whole hour to do my homework and chores. Is that okay, Ma?" he added, glancing at her for approval.

"That's fine, honey."

"Hey, Ma, maybe Lucas can stay for dinner? You can make your world famous burgers on the grill, with homemade French fries and stuff. What do you say, Ma? Huh? Is it okay?"

She saw the hope and joy shining in her son's eyes and hated to disappoint him, but she also had to be practical. She still had more boxes packed then unpacked and finding anything in the mess would be nothing short of a miracle.

"Honey, I haven't even unpacked or set up the grill yet—"

"That's okay," Rusty said hurriedly. "Maybe Lucas and I could do it?" Pleading eyes turned to Lucas. "I mean, isn't that the kind of thing uh…a buddy does? Help another buddy maybe unpack and set stuff up?" he asked with a shrug, making Lucas smile.

"You're absolutely right, Rusty," Lucas agreed. "That's exactly what a buddy should do." He looked at Katie. "How about if Rusty and I unpack and set up the grill tomorrow after school. After his homework and chores," he clarified, letting his gaze shift back to Rusty, who nodded in silent agreement.

Katie looked from her son's expectant face to Lucas and forgot all the things she'd already had scheduled for tomorrow. So she'd simply add one more to the growing list. "All right. As long as it's not an imposition on Lucas," she added meaningfully.

"Is it?" Rusty felt obliged to ask and Lucas shook his head.

"No, it'll be just fine. Besides, I think it's something every male should know how to do."

"What? Finagle someone else to do your work for you?" Katie asked with a grin, making Lucas chuckle.

"No, set up a grill. I think it will be good experience for Rusty."

"All right." Katie hesitated. "I'll stop at the store on my way home, and get the fixings for burgers and fries. If you guys set up the grill, I'll do the cooking."

"Awesome."

"And thank you for the invitation, Rusty," Lucas said. "I appreciate it."

"You're welcome."

"Okay, inside for a shower and then bed," Katie ordered. "I'll be in in a minute to tuck you in."

"Ma!" Mortified, Rusty rolled his eyes. "I'm too old to be tucked in," he said, nodding his head toward Lucas and flushing pink.

"Oh, yes, that's right," Katie said solemnly, giving him a nod. "Now that you're at an advanced age of eleven, you're far too old to be tucked into bed by your old mother."

"Right." Grinning, Rusty gave them both another wave. "See you." He pulled open the screen door, then pushed open the front door, and let both slam behind him.

Katie sighed. "He's growing up so fast," she said wistfully as she climbed the rest of the stairs to stand on the front porch. "Sometimes it's hard to believe he's almost a teenager." With a sigh, she leaned against the porch railing. "The time seems to be just flying by."

Lucas laughed, following her up the stairs. "That has to be the scariest word in the English language, at least for parents."

"What?" She turned to him. He'd joined her on the porch and was leaning against the railing as well.

"Teenager," Lucas said, reaching out to brush a stray strand of hair off her cheek.

Katie froze at his touch. She hadn't realized he'd moved so close, and his touch, his closeness, seemed to make her pulse do a wicked dance.

"I…agree," she stammered, realizing when he'd stroked his finger down her cheek, it felt as if she'd been touched by a live wire, and her skin, her heart and her pulse were all still singing.

"I…I…" She had to swallow. She'd remember what she was going to say in a moment. She was certain of it.

But he was looking at her in a way that left her feeling very vulnerable and exposed. And very, very needy.

And he was standing just a fraction too close, close enough she could smell his faint masculine scent, feel the warmth of his body, a warmth that seemed to be clouding her mind and tangling her tongue while still drawing her closer to him.

"Katie." Lucas moved closer still, drawn by something far more powerful than his own thoughts and fears. He told himself he should be careful, wary, but his mind ignored the caution.

She was so near, her scent swirling around him,

heady and feminine, making him long and ache in a way he couldn't ever remember.

The urge, the need to touch her, to taste her, was so strong he was certain he might go mad if he didn't satisfy the desire.

He slid his hands to her slender waist, noting her eyes widen into saucers. He smiled, wondering if she knew how much she looked like her son at the moment with her eyes wide, hopeful, expectant, curious and maybe just a bit frightened.

"Lucas." She lifted her hands to his chest, telling herself it was to stop him. To keep him at bay.

But it was a lie, and she knew it. His mouth hovered a mere inches from hers, making her yearn somewhere deep inside, yearn and want, two things she'd told herself she could never allow again.

She was going to push him away, she told herself, and try to grab her sanity before it fled once again. Then she looked into his gaze and lost her train of thought.

With her mind blank and her senses on alert, she tilted her head up just as he lowered his. She felt her breath flutter out on a dreamy sigh as his lips brushed gently against her.

Katie tried to tell herself she was going to push him away. To stop him. In just a moment.

His mouth was warm and firm, and coaxed hers gently into responding. Her lips opened greedily for his, as if she were drowning and only his touch would save her.

Her mind emptied totally as the world spun around

her, under her, whirling and whirling as if she'd stepped on a Tilt-A-Whirl.

She gripped the front of his shirt for balance as heat and desire snaked through her, slowly, thoroughly, arousing every sleeping nerve until her entire body ached and she arched against Lucas, fitting her softness to the masculine hardness of him, trying to put out the fire his touch seemed to have brought blazing back to life.

A moan escaped her as he deepened the kiss, as his touch circled, then danced with hers in a mating ritual as old as time. She went with it, allowing Lucas and his kiss to sweep sanity and sense from her mind until nothing filled her but the need and desire his touch aroused.

His hands tightened around her waist as hers rose to slide through the silk of his hair, to cling, fearing she might fall off the earth if she didn't hold onto him.

Another soft moan filtered through the air and Lucas realized it was he who'd moaned. He'd expected Katie to be cool, to be reserved. Nothing had prepared him for the blast of feminine heat that roared through him, licking at him like he was little more than dry timber the moment their lips met and clung.

Her scent swirled around him, drowning him in a sea where the only thing he was aware of was her. Her taste. Her scent. Her touch. Her. Just her.

He drew her even closer, not wanting even a breath separating them. Instinctively he knew that one kiss would never satisfy the gnawing need that Katie had awakened. Needs he thought long dead and buried. Needs he knew better than to acknowledge or want.

He had to think, to clear his head, to remember why

he couldn't and shouldn't be doing this. Remember the risk he was taking, with his own heart, as well as hers.

"Lucas." His name whispered out of her mouth as she drew back, her eyes huge and frightened in her pale face. She would have tumbled right back into the porch railing if he hadn't had his arms around her. Her legs felt as if they couldn't hold her, and she sagged against him breathless and slightly dizzy from the intensity of their kiss.

"Thank you for sharing your son with me tonight," he said softly, managing a smile even though his insides were rioting. Gently, he ran a shaky finger down her nose, knowing it was better to say nothing than to say something he'd regret, now, when his mind was clouded by desire, by passion and all he wanted to do was drag her back in his arms again. "I'll see you tomorrow, Katie."

He stepped back, needed to put some necessary distance between them, and jogged down the stairs, not certain who was more shaken by their kiss. Him. Or her. If he didn't know better he'd swear his legs were shaking.

"Good night, Lucas," she called softly, holding onto the porch railing for balance as she watched him walk away. "Thank you."

She waited, watching until he was out of sight before going inside the house. She shut and locked the front door, then leaned against it and closed her eyes.

She needed a moment, she realized, just a moment to settle herself. The last thing she wanted was for her son to see her this confused and at odds. She still had to go in and kiss Rusty good-night and she just needed a moment to pull herself together.

Pressing a hand to her racing heart, Katie realized she'd been weak and foolish. Allowing herself to have such ridiculous fantasies about Lucas and what had just happened between them.

It was a kiss—nothing more, nothing less, she told herself. And certainly no reason to get herself all in a tizzy.

She'd kissed men in the years since Jed's death. Lots of them.

She scowled. Okay, so maybe it was only two, and since one was her uncle and that was a chaste kiss on the cheek, it probably didn't count.

Her kiss with Lucas left her breathless, aching and wanting more.

But she couldn't have more, she realized. And even entertaining the idea of having more with Lucas was both foolish and foolhardy. And could only lead to heartbreak.

She was a single mother of an almost teenaged child, far too old and mature to be spinning fantasies about happily-ever-after simply because a man kissed her.

And she'd do well to remember that.

She had a well-ordered life filled with more responsibilities than any sane woman could handle, not just to her son and her mother, but to the paper and her community, not to mention the responsibilities she had to herself.

She didn't have time to be mooning over some man

like she was a fickle, free young woman without a care in the world or a thought on the planet.

She'd been that carefree woman once, and learned just how fast carefree could turn into concern when life tossed you an unexpected curve.

She'd barely survived the first time. She wasn't about to risk her heart or her son's heart a second time.

No, she was older and much smarter now, she told herself, patting her still scrambling heart. Now she knew exactly what could happen if she wasn't responsible, if she wasn't reliable, if she didn't do exactly what her obligations demanded of her.

And the thought of going through the grief and fear and worry again that she'd just gone through over the past six years simply terrified her.

So she'd never risk having her heart, or Rusty's, broken ever again.

With a sigh, Katie rubbed her throbbing forehead. She suddenly had a ferocious headache. Probably because she was so blasted tired. It had been a long day, and she had to admit, a long night. She should have come home earlier so she could unpack some more boxes and get ready for the new work day.

Instead, she'd chosen to be careless and spend her evening with a man she had no business having the kinds of thoughts she was having about.

Well, at least no harm had come from one evening, she reasoned. Besides, it was *just* a kiss, she told herself, and even if her insides were still churning like jelly, and even if her heart felt as if it were racing to some imaginary finish line, she had to get a grip and keep it on her heart. And her mind.

Lucas Porter was no more interested in her than she was in him. It was her son, she reminded herself, that he was trying to help. It was her son he'd so kindly and generously offered to spend time with—not her. And she'd do well to remember that.

As Katie walked through the house, turning off lights and locking up, she tried to banish Lucas from her mind.

But as she headed toward her own bedroom, Lucas's taste lingered on her lips, and thoughts of him lingered fitfully in her mind.

Chapter Five

"**I**'m late, I know, I know," Katie said as she dashed into the newspaper office the next morning, her arms full. "I'm hideously late and I'm sorry, it couldn't be helped." She stopped and pressed a hand to her racing heart to catch her breath. "We had an emergency this morning. A basketball emergency," she clarified when Lindsey's brows lifted in question. "Rusty realized at the last minute that basketball practice starts today. And we couldn't find his shoes. I think I unpacked twenty boxes before we found them."

And she was already exhausted. Thoughts and dreams of Lucas had disturbed her sleep all night. She'd spent more time tossing and turning than sleeping, and now, she felt more tired than she had when she went to bed last night.

She couldn't remember any other male she'd tried to

treat like a "brother" disturbing her sleep quite so much. But then again, she mused, trying to hide a smile, she couldn't remember another man she'd treated like a "brother" kissing her senseless, either.

"Good morning to you, too," Lindsey said, giving her a look. "Now, I hate to be the bearer of more bad tidings, but I don't think your day's going to get better any time soon, Katie." Lindsey turned back to her desk and picked up a stack of pink message slips, fanning them out in the air for Katie to see and frown over. "These are all for you. From your mother," Lindsey said pointedly, eyeing Katie over the rim of her thick glasses. "Your mother is on a rip-roaring tear about something. And apparently you're at the heart of it."

"I know, I know," Katie admitted with a sigh, heading toward her office to dump her stuff. "I think Patience told her I was being rude to the police chief last night."

Fascinated, Lindsey followed Katie into her office. "Now why on earth would that woman tell your mother something like that?" she demanded with a scowl.

"Because that's what we told her—Patience, I mean," Katie absently explained as she dug through the piles of papers and folders on her desk to find what she needed for her meeting with Lucas this morning.

"Well, for goodness sake why on earth—who's *we?*" Lindsey asked abruptly, her brows rising in surprise as she caught that last phrase.

"Lucas and I." Smiling at the memory, Katie tucked her notes and files into her arm and looked at Lindsey, then sighed. "We went out for pizza last night. And no, don't look like that. It wasn't a date—"

"Uh-huh."

"No, really," Katie insisted with a grin, realizing she was probably going to have to explain this more than once today. Maybe she ought to just print her explanation on the front page of this week's newspaper, that way she could be sure *everyone* in town read it. "Lucas is Rusty's Buddy—you know, the Buddy for a Boy program?"

"Uh-huh," Lindsey said with a slow nod, suspicion still clouding her eyes. "I understand all about the Buddy program, Katie. I wrote the blasted article for your uncle explaining it in the newspaper. But what I don't understand is what the Buddy program and you and Lucas going out for pizza—together," she added with a great deal more emphasis than necessary, "has to do with one another. And then of course why anyone would tell Patience Pettibone anything is beyond me."

"Lucas is Rusty's buddy," Katie explained patiently. "Lucas invited Rusty for pizza and they invited me to come along." Katie shrugged, trying to dismiss the significance of last night. "It was a way for them to get to know one another and yet allow me to be there as a buffer."

"A buffer, huh?" Lindsey repeated shrewdly. "Okay, got it," she said with a nod. "If that's the official story you're going with, well, hell, I can repeat it just as good as you can." She turned and headed back to her own desk, muttering under her breath. "It wasn't a date. You were merely a buffer." Lindsey was almost to her desk before she stopped abruptly. "Wait a minute," she said, whirling around to face Katie again as she tried to sneak toward the front door to make her escape. "What does you being a buffer for Rusty have to do with you being rude to the police chief?" Lindsey demanded, planting her hands on her hips. "And why on earth would you tell Patience—the Paul Revere of Cooper's Cove— about it?"

Katie sighed. "I wasn't really rude to the chief, but we figured if we didn't tell Patience something, by this morning she'd have spread it all over town that Lucas and I were seen at the pizza parlor. Together."

Confused, Lindsey scratched her head. "But you were with Lucas at the pizza parlor, weren't you?"

"Well, yes," Katie admitted, biting her lip and glancing at the clock again. "But it wasn't a date, remember?"

"Oh, yeah, it was that buffer thing," Lindsey said with another knowing nod. "Now I get it. *Not*," she added with a scowl, making Katie laugh again.

"It's really a long story, Lindsey, and if I don't leave now, I'm going to be late for my morning meeting with the chief." She waved a sheaf of folders and papers at Lindsey. "Remember, the street closings for the Halloween carnival? My 'Police Beat' column for next week? And the special safety letter from the chief for the Halloween issue?"

"Yeah, yeah, I know," Lindsey said with a wave of her hand. "I'm the one who briefed you yesterday, remember?" Her brows drew together. "But what am I supposed to tell your mother when she calls back for the…uh…" She quickly counted the message slips. "Tenth time?"

"Tell her I'm out doing an interview and I'll call her later. I need to talk to her anyway."

"You're a brave woman, Katherine," Lindsey said

with a slow shake of her head, pushing up her thick glasses. It was no secret that Lindsey was a tad intimidated by Katie's mother, not to mention Katie's supposedly psychic Aunt Gracie.

Ever since her mother had read Lindsey's astrology charts fifteen years ago and accurately predicted a tornado that would hit just outside of town, narrowly missing Lindsey's house, which Katie's mother had insisted Lindsey evacuate before there was even the thought or threat of a tornado, Lindsey had tried to steer clear of Louella simply because Katie's mother's astrological predictions and Katie's Aunt Gracie's psychic predictions totally spooked Lindsey.

Ten years ago when Katie's aunt had charged into the newspaper office, demanding Lindsey call off her wedding to Frankie Flannigan, the fire chief's "bad boy" brother, or else get her heart broken, Lindsey had been furious and appalled, until the next week when her fiancé had run off with another woman.

Since then all this "new-age stuff," as Lindsey referred to it, was far too much for her Midwestern practical self. She was convinced Lady Louella and Gracie had some kind of special powers, powers that scared the dickens out of her.

It never failed to amuse Katie that Lindsey, someone who was so levelheaded and practical on every other issue, could be spooked by *her* mother. Or her sweet, unusual little aunt.

"I'll tell her, but I'm warning you, Katie, your mama better not put any strange curse on me. Her sister, neither," Lindsey warned with a shake of her finger.

Katie laughed. "Don't worry, Lindsey. Mama's saving all her curses for the mayor."

"Thank the Lord," Lindsey said with a relieved sigh, making Katie laugh again as she headed toward the door again. "Not that the man doesn't deserve it," she mumbled as an afterthought.

"I'll be back as soon as I can." Katie pushed open the door, then said over her shoulder. "Oh, and do me a favor, Lindsey? Call Mr. Hensen at the butcher shop and ask him if he can grind a sirloin steak for me. Tell him I'll need about two pounds and to grind it twice. I'll pick it up on my way home. I might be late, so tell him I'll just ring his back door when I get there." She gave Lindsey a weak smile. "Rusty wants burgers on the grill, tonight."

"Two pounds worth, huh?" Lindsey said, pretending to be intensely interested in the messages in her hand. "Say hi to the chief for me," she added with a smile as Katie sailed out the door. "Sure hope he likes ground sirloin burgers."

Lucas was just hanging up the phone when his administrative assistant waved Katie through to his office.

She hesitated in the doorway for a moment, and just looked at him. He was just so gorgeous, she thought with a dreamy sigh. And she had to admit she sure liked looking at him. Kissing him wasn't bad, either, she mused, thinking about last night.

Today he was dressed in immaculately pressed jeans, boots and a Cooper's Cove police department khaki uniform shirt. All members of the department were required to wear the shirt to let the public know they were police officers. He had a shoulder holster with a weapon that she was pretty sure he'd never even have to remove, at least not in this town.

Katie couldn't help but wonder if that dull brown shirt looked as good on everyone as it did on Lucas, with his broad shoulders and slender hips.

"Hi," she said with a smile, suddenly feeling nervous and a bit tongue-tied, simply because she was all but ogling the man again.

His grin matched hers. "Hi yourself. Come on in," he said. "I know we have a meeting this morning, but I might have to cut it short, I'm afraid." His smile was apologetic. "I have a luncheon date."

Katie could almost feel the smile freeze on her face as her stomach dropped.

"A lunch date," she repeated dully. Nodding, she headed toward the chair opposite his desk. "How lovely," she said, her voice slightly strained as she dropped into the chair like a stone.

There was no reason on earth for her to be jealous, she scolded herself, recognizing the flash of hot fire burning in her gut for exactly what it was. Lucas was a single, eligible man in a town where single men were generally over sixty and cranky.

A young, gorgeous eligible man was a rare commodity. So of course he'd date. He'd no doubt have his pick of any single female in town.

So why was she so surprised?

More importantly, why on earth was she jealous?

It was utterly ridiculous, she told herself as she pretended to flip through her notes and files, fearing her strained emotions might show on her face. She had no claim on Lucas, and didn't want one, she reminded herself.

She was a perfectly happy, content single mom with more than enough responsibilities to keep her going. She certainly didn't need a man to complicate her life or her son's.

"Maybe we'd better get started," Katie said, pulling free last year's list of street closings and leaning forward in her chair to hand it to Lucas. "This needs to be updated," she informed him. "It's the list of all the streets that will be closed for the Halloween carnival next month. I need you to look it over and update it so we can print it for the next four weeks until the carnival. I'm sorry, Lucas, but I'll need that back by end of day tomorrow."

Looking at the article, Lucas nodded absently. "Will do. I take it the Halloween carnival is a big deal around here?"

Katie laughed. "Every holiday around here is a big deal, but especially the Halloween carnival and the Christmas festival. They're like the granddaddies of all carnivals for this town. We have food vendors, games of chance, carnival rides, clowns, and my mom and my aunt set up their own little 'New Age' booth where they read palms, tell fortunes and horoscopes. And almost every business in town either sponsors a booth or sets up their own. All proceeds go toward afterschool programs, which is why everyone tries to pitch in and do their share."

"You don't really believe in all that, do you?" Lucas asked, looking up at her with a smile. "The astrology and psychic stuff I mean?"

"I guess I don't *disbelieve* it," she admitted with a smile. "I've been living with my mom and aunt and their…talents, so to speak, for my whole life. Truthfully, I don't even pay much attention to it anymore." Katie frowned suddenly. "Unless my Aunt Gracie does something or says something totally off the wall or out of the blue." Katie shook her head and laughed. "That tends to spook me. And she has been known to do that. Sometimes she 'gets things,' but not all at one time. She always says it's like a television picture going in and out, and then getting blurry. And unfortunately, Aunt Gracie has a tendency to blurt things out before she gets the 'whole picture,' so to speak, and that can be a bit disconcerting."

"I imagine it would." A man could really lose himself in that face of hers, Lucas mused, trying to listen to Katie's words and not get lost in her beauty.

This morning that hair of hers, that gorgeous silky hair that made him itch to slide his hands through, was in a bit of disarray and looked as if it were about to tumble off its perch atop her head. Why she didn't just pull out the pins and let it free was a mystery. Her hair was one of her most attractive features. Along with her eyes, her lips, her face. Lucas sighed. And of course that gorgeous, ultra-sexy body that today was clothed in her usual crisp, pressed jeans and white blouse.

"One morning shortly after I got married, I opened the front door to get the morning newspaper and found Aunt Gracie standing on the front porch in her nightgown, barefoot," Kate said.

"Was she hurt?" Lucas asked with a frown, grateful

he'd managed to follow the conversation, even though just being near Katie distracted all rational thought.

Katie shook her head. "No. She wasn't hurt, but I was running in a marathon that day. Aunt Gracie refused to come in the house, refused to go home, refused to do anything until I promised her I wouldn't run that day. She just kept saying it would jostle the boy and make him mad."

"The boy?" Lucas repeated with a confused frown.

"Yep. The boy."

"And you thought…what? That she'd gone round the bend?" Lucas asked with a warm smile, and Katie nodded.

"Right. It just didn't make any sense to me and I didn't know what boy she was talking about, but I couldn't run, not when she was so upset about it." Katie shrugged. "I kind of dismissed it until the following week—when I fainted dead away in the butcher shop while shopping for dinner. I scared poor Mr. Hensen half to death. Thankfully, Dr. Robsen was having lunch in the diner and someone ran to get him. By the time I came to, I was looking up at half the town, who were grinning like loons because Dr. Robsen had told everyone his diagnosis before I'd even woken up." She laughed at the memory. "Aunt Gracie really got a kick out of that and told Dr. Robsen he was a little late, that she'd already told me I was expecting a baby boy the week before, which was news to me. But I guess in her own roundabout way Aunt Gracie did tell me I was expecting a boy. I just didn't connect the dots."

"Ahh," Lucas said in acknowledgment. "That's the boy she was talking about?"

"Yeah, turned out it was Rusty," Katie admitted with a chuckle. "But let's just say Aunt Gracie's version was subject to interpretation, or maybe translation is a better word. Anyway, she couldn't understand why I was so surprised at the news since she thought she'd already told me, but since I didn't have a clue what she was talking about at the time…" Katie's voice trailed off and she shrugged. "I don't do…gibberish very well I'm afraid. So since then, like I said, I don't necessarily believe, but I don't disbelieve in it, either."

"I'll make sure to remember that."

Aware that he was pressed for time, Katie pulled another folder loose from the pile on her lap. "These are copies of the weekly 'Police Beat' column the newspaper runs. Every week I meet with the police chief and we discuss any crimes or problems from the prior week."

"I can't imagine there's enough crime in town to warrant one column, let alone a year's worth." The worst crime he'd encountered since he'd taken over was old Mrs. Hennighan forgetting which house was hers and wandering into others.

Or the local teens making a pathetic attempt to drag race down the measly two-block area that comprised Main Street.

But he hardly thought that was worthy of being written up in the newspaper.

"It's not just to report crimes, Lucas. The column is also a tool for you to speak directly to all the residents on a somewhat personal level. I think it will help bridge the gap as you get to know people. Believe it or not, just from reading that column, people will form an opinion of you and feel as if they already know you whether they do or not."

He nodded. "Okay, but what kinds of things go in this 'Police Beat' column?"

Katie thought about it for a moment. "Well, last spring for example, the last week of school, during finals, the police chief wrote an article explaining it was the last week of school and finals were in progress, which meant students wouldn't be coming and going at the usual times, so drivers should be particularly aware that children could be coming out or going into the school all during the day. And possibly riding their bikes, skateboards, or even just on foot, so he wanted every driver to pay particular attention while in the school zone."

"That's an excellent idea, Katie," Lucas said, nodding his head. "I think a friendly reminder that cars and drivers have to share the road with others can't be repeated too often." He opened the folder. "Let me review some of the articles and let you know when I come up with an idea for next week's column, unless you already have something in mind?" he asked, glancing up at her.

"Please, I have enough trouble coming up with ideas for my own columns, let alone others. Feel free to write about anything you want."

"Will do. Now when do you need this article?"

"I'm afraid I'll need it no later than a week from today." She leaned forward, then hesitated, wanting to be helpful, but not intrusive. "Lucas, sometimes if someone hasn't had much experience writing they sort of go brain-dead when they start, especially knowing they need a certain number of words in a certain period of time."

"Now you are scaring me," Lucas said with a laugh.

"Sorry, I didn't mean to." She paused for a moment. "I guess the best advice I can give you is to merely write in the same conversational tone you talk in. Keep it friendly and informal—informational, but not preachy."

"Are you sure you don't want to write this?" he asked, and she held up her hands.

"No, thanks. I've got enough on my plate right now." She pulled one more file loose from her pile. "Now, there's just one more thing and then I'll let you get back to work." She glanced up at him and felt her heart tumble over at the way he was looking at her. "I do a column every week called 'Getting to Know You.' It's probably the most personal and popular column in town. Each week I interview a resident of the town and ask questions that maybe no one has ever thought of asking. It's a way for the town to get to really know more about their citizens and a way for the citizens to sort of connect with the community." She hesitated for a moment, gathering her courage. Considering the reaction she'd gotten the first night they'd met, when he'd learned she was a reporter and accused her of snooping, she had no idea how he'd react to an official request for an interview. "I was wondering if you'd give me an interview for next week's column? Since you're new in town I thought it would be a fabulous way for everyone in town to get to know you."

She had no idea why she was suddenly so nervous.

Maybe because she had a gut feeling that Lucas wasn't going to like this idea, wasn't going to like the idea of her asking him questions—*personal* questions.

She had a horrible feeling he was going to think she was merely *snooping* again when nothing could be further from the truth.

While she'd admit to herself she was curious about his past, curious about a great many things about Lucas and his life before he came to Cooper's Cove, that didn't mean she wanted to start snooping or prying into his life or his business.

She'd always felt that if any relationship, even a friendship, was to grow and prosper there had to be trust between the people involved. Without trust, there could never be any kind of relationship, simply because all relationships had to be built on the solid foundation of mutual trust.

And if Lucas didn't trust her enough to give her an interview, to answer questions about his past, then what?

She honestly didn't know, which was probably why she found herself holding her breath.

"Katie." He only said her name, but the tone of his voice set off alarm bells inside of her. "Do you mind if I shut my door so we can talk privately?"

"Uh….no. Not at all," she said, clutching her files and folders with nervous hands. Private. He wanted to talk in private so maybe he was finally going to talk to her about himself, his past, about all the things that any woman would naturally be curious about, especially a woman who found her young son smitten with the man, to say nothing about the amount of time Lucas would be spending with Rusty.

She wanted to know this information for Rusty's sake, she told herself. She had a responsibility as a parent to make certain she knew everything about the adults her son associated with and she didn't think it was unreasonable for her to want to know more about Lucas's background.

It was simply parental common sense.

But from the look on his face as he rounded his desk and quietly shut his office door, she didn't think he was going to see it that way.

When he shut the door, all sound from the outer offices and hallways was instantly silenced, and it seemed as if they were suddenly alone in the world.

And Katie wished the idea of being all alone with him didn't make her so...twitchy.

Instead of retreating back behind his desk, Lucas grabbed the empty chair next to her, pulled it closer and turned it so he was facing her, then sat down.

For a moment, he said nothing. He merely looked at her until she was certain she was going to start fidgeting under his riveting gaze. There was something intensely male about that look of his, Katie mused, something that made her respond and feel on a level that was instinctively primal and entirely female.

Perhaps that's why just being around him unnerved her so.

"Katie," he finally said, reaching for one of her damp hands and cradling it in his own. "I think it's very important for us to keep these relationships separate, so to speak."

"Separate?" She shook her head as he gently stroked the skin of her hand with his thumb. "I'm sorry. I don't understand what you mean."

"Let's see if I can explain this." He hesitated a moment as if gathering his thoughts. "In our professional lives, I'm the chief of police, and you're a reporter and the managing editor of the town's only newspaper."

She couldn't help but smile. "Well, thank you for pointing that out, Lucas, but I wasn't really confused about our titles or roles."

"Well that's what I want to talk to you about. Our roles. Everyone plays different roles depending on who they're with and the circumstances. When I'm with Rusty, acting as his buddy, I'm not the police chief any more than when you're at home, supervising his homework, you're not acting as a reporter, but as his mother. I guess what I'm saying is that I think it's vitally important for Rusty's sake, and for our own, that we keep our professional and personal lives separate."

"I don't think I understand, Lucas." She blew out a breath, feeling a thread of annoyance begin to unravel. "I don't know how to separate myself. One minute a reporter. One minute a mother. I'm both of those things at the same time." And had worked damn hard to be able to do both well.

"True, just as I'm the chief and Rusty's buddy at the same time. But it's very important that we not let anything that happens say…in our professional lives, any disagreements or differences of opinion we have in our professional lives interfere in our personal lives. I think to do so might end up hurting Rusty, something I don't think either of us want to do."

"Okay," Katie began slowly, desperately trying to understand what he was saying by all the things he *wasn't* saying. "If I understand you correctly, what you're saying is that we can't let anything that happens in our professional lives affect the way we relate in our personal lives as it pertains to Rusty, right?"

"No," Lucas said slowly, meeting her confused gaze. "As it relates to *anything,* not just Rusty."

Katie nodded, a sense of dread unfolding inside. She had a feeling she already knew what the bottom line of all of this was, and she wasn't particularly happy about it.

"This is your way of saying you're not going to let me interview you for the 'Getting to Know You' column, isn't it? And as the managing editor of the newspaper, you don't want me to hold it against you or let my feelings about your refusal impact your position as Rusty's buddy? Have I got this right?"

He nodded. He couldn't tell her that there was no way he could bare his soul and the horrendous scars of his past to anyone, let alone a reporter. It just was never going to happen, no matter what the reasons.

He had a powerful distrust of the press—and was wary of the power they wielded. Reporters were masters of shaping words to tell the story they wanted to tell, regardless of the truth, or how it impacted the people they were writing about.

He'd been burned so many times after his family's death, burned by the press and their desire to get a story simply to boost their ratings. At times, they made up their facts, using bits and pieces of the truth, and huge fragments of lies.

So why one earth would he ever want to give another interview? It wouldn't heal his scars, or bring back his family, or lighten the guilt he'd carried around for so long now he feared it had become a permanent part of him.

He had nothing to gain. And everything to lose. He'd moved to Cooper's Cove to get a fresh start, to try to put the past behind him and start anew.

So why would he invite a reporter to start digging into his life all over again?

There simply was no sense or point to it.

But from the look on Katie's face, trying to get her to understand his reasons without actually telling her his motives was going to be difficult.

So he chose his words carefully. "I don't want my refusal to do an interview with you to affect or impact my relationship with Rusty. I don't think that would be fair to him. Not giving interviews—ever—is a personal choice and a private matter. It has nothing whatsoever to do with my being Rusty's buddy. Or, quite frankly, with you as Rusty's mother. Do you understand that?" He waited until she nodded, but clearly she still wasn't convinced. "Katie, it wouldn't matter who the managing editor or the reporter asking was, I wouldn't give them an interview under any circumstances. It goes against my own personal policy. So I guess what I'm saying is just because you happen to be both Rusty's mom and the managing editor, I don't want one to prejudice or influence the other. I plan on spending a lot of time with

Rusty, and as his mother it's only natural that some of that time will also be spent with you. It could be very uncomfortable for all of us if we allow our professional disagreements or differences to interfere with our personal relationships."

"Lucas, do you really think I'd let your refusal to give me an interview interfere in your relationship with my son?" She stared at him curiously, desperately trying not to be hurt. "Do you think so little of me that you don't think I can separate my responsibilities for my son's well-being from my responsibilities to the paper?"

"Katie," he said, his voice husky as he reached for her other hand and held both tightly. "This honestly has nothing to do with *you*. I hope you believe me on that. I truly believe you are a responsible, respectful, ethical professional. And probably very good at your job."

"I am," she confirmed proudly.

"But as I told you last night, I believe in keeping my private life just that—private. And I guess what I'm asking is for you to accept my feelings about this, and not let it color your judgment toward me about being Rusty's buddy. One really doesn't have anything to do with the other."

"Lucas, do you really think that's totally fair? I understand that you want your privacy. I understand that you want to keep your personal life to yourself. But think about something. If you had a son, would you want someone you barely knew, who refused to tell you anything about his private life, spending time with him?"

His face changed. In an instant it drained of color and she knew she'd hit some kind of nerve. The problem was she didn't quite know which one. He'd already told her last night he didn't have any children. So why was he so secretive about his personal life? And why did the mere mention of his having a son make his face go white?

In her experience as a reporter, and as a woman, anyone who refused to tell you something usually was trying to hide something.

So what was Lucas hiding?

And more importantly, why?

Katie mentally shook her head. She didn't know, but as a mother, she knew she had a responsibility to find out.

"Katie, for goodness sakes," he finally said. "I'm the police chief. Not some stranger Rusty hustled in off the street. Do you have any idea the kind of vetting process I had to go through to become chief? Do you have any idea what kind of background check I had to go through just to get a gun permit in this state? If I had any deep, dark secrets or a criminal record, I'd never have made it past the first interview for this job. I can give you as many professional character witnesses as you want or need to feel comfortable if that's the road you want to go, but believe me when I tell you, your son will always be safe with me." His eyes darkened and his jaw clenched. "I will always guard your son's life as if it were my own. You have my word on it." His gaze pleaded with her to understand, and she wanted to, but she simply couldn't.

"Lucas," she began carefully. "I wish I could say I understand why you won't allow an interview, but I don't. However," she continued when his face darkened a bit, "maybe I don't have to understand it. It's really not my business. You're entitled to keep your private life just that—private. But I think it's important for you to know and understand that I do *totally and completely believe you* when you say Rusty will always be safe with you. The thought that he'd be anything else never crossed my mind."

"Good." Lucas finally smiled at her. "Thank you, Katie, that means a lot to me."

"And even though I might not like or understand your reasons for not wanting to discuss your private life with the managing editor of the newspaper, I promise that I will do my best not to let my feelings about that interfere in any way with any personal relationship you have with my son. Or with me. I hardly think you'd be an effective buddy if Rusty's mother threw rocks at you every time you came near the house," she said, trying to make him smile, and grateful when she finally succeeded. "Even though Rusty will tell you I throw like a girl, and I can't see two feet in front of me without my glasses, who knows, I might get a lucky toss in and then where would we be?" She could see the tension ease out of him, see his shoulders relax, his jaw unclench.

But she also saw something else, something that nibbled away at her far more than her curiosity—she saw pain in Lucas's eyes.

It made her heart ache in a way it hadn't in a very long time to know that something or someone had caused that terrible pain she saw in his eyes.

It made her want to just wrap her arms around him and hold him close, to soothe and comfort in a way she hadn't done with a man in a very long time. And until this moment, until she'd been face-to-face with the naked, raw pain in Lucas's face, she hadn't realized she'd wanted to comfort a man again.

But she did.

And she hadn't a clue what to do with those feelings.

"Thank you, Katie." Slowly, he lifted her hand again and gently brushed a kiss across every fingertip, making her pulse hammer and her heart seem to skip a beat. "You have no idea how much that means to me."

Because her pulse was scampering, Katie glanced up and saw the time. "Oh my goodness, Lucas!" She jumped to her feet. "It's after twelve, I've got to go. I've got a million things to do today." She began gathering her files and folders up.

"And if I don't hustle I'm going to be late for my date with your mother."

Katie froze. "My mother?" she repeated, turning to look at him. "You have a *date* with my mother?"

He chuckled, bending to pick up a few papers she'd dropped from her folders. "Well, that's what she called it this morning when she called and invited me to lunch." The sadness had lifted from his eyes and now mischief once again danced freely. "Apparently someone tattled and told her that last night you were seen fighting with the police chief in front of the whole town." Slowly, Lucas shook his head. "Imagine that?" he said, trying to keep a straight face as she groaned.

"Remind me to strangle Patience Pettibone when I see her," Katie muttered in annoyance. He laughed, dropping an arm around her shoulder as she started walking toward the door. The warmth of him pressed the entire length of her and she felt that odd yearning deep inside again.

"Uh…maybe I'd better remind you that you're talking to a duly sworn officer of the law."

"Details, details," she muttered.

"By the way, when you see Rusty's mother—"

"Rusty's mother?" Katie repeated, glancing up at him in confusion. Then she saw his smile, and got it. Rusty's buddy wanted to talk to Rusty's mom. "Okay. When I see Rusty's mother…what?"

"Tell her that she probably shouldn't rush home tonight since Rusty's planning a little surprise for her."

"Surprise?"

Lucas nodded, and the look on his face made her immediately suspicious.

"Does this surprise have anything to do with spitting contests or anything else gross like that?"

Lucas burst out laughing. "Not a thing. Scout's honor," he said, crossing his heart with his free hand.

"Okay. But I have a message for Rusty's buddy as well."

"And what would that message be?"

"Rusty forgot that the first basketball practice is today. So he's going to be an hour later for everything than he'd originally planned."

"That's right," Lucas said as he paused in the doorway, his arms still around Katie's shoulder. "I forgot about that." He grinned at her confusion. "I volunteered to help out the coach with the team. I guess I'd better start checking that planner my assistant keeps writing things down in."

"Sounds like a plan to me." She glanced up at him and immediately thought about last night and the kiss they shared. If she stood just on her tiptoes she could brush her lips across his.

Right. All she needed was to have someone report *that* to her mother!

"I better go," she finally stammered, realizing she'd better step away from him before she did something to embarrass both of them. "I'll…uh…see you later." Katie bolted toward the elevator, stepping in and then turning to watch Lucas, their gazes meeting and holding until the doors slowly closed.

Sixty minutes later Katie was in her office, desperately trying to proofread the final blue lines—those were the final, typeset pages that, when printed, would become the actual newspaper.

The printer sent over the blue lines two days before the newspaper was actually printed and she had exactly eight hours to correct any errors before delivering them back to the printer before 8:00 p.m. the same day. Any errors she didn't find would end up in the newspaper and she'd hear about them from everyone in town for a full week, until next week's edition came out.

At the rate she was going today, running behind since she woke up, she was going to have a difficult time making her deadline.

And if she didn't make her deadline, the printer wouldn't have the newspaper ready for distribution on Friday afternoon. Something that had never happened in the history of Cooper's Cove, something she wasn't about to let happen today.

She *had* to make that deadline.

So she tried to put all thoughts of Lucas out of her mind and simply concentrate on what she was doing. But when she found herself reading the same paragraph for the fourth time, and still not knowing what it said, she realized she needed a break.

Her curiosity had been aroused by all the things Lucas refused to tell her about his private life, all the things that her mind was imagining. And now she simply couldn't stop thinking about it.

Or Lucas.

What on earth could have happened in his past that he was so adamant about protecting? Or hiding?

She didn't know, but she did know that she couldn't betray the fledgling trust they'd developed, a trust that was absolutely paramount to Lucas's relationship with Rusty.

She couldn't do anything that would jeopardize her son's relationship with Lucas, or Rusty would never forgive her. And, she thought with a sigh, she wouldn't blame him because if that happened, knowing how much Rusty was looking forward to having Lucas as his buddy, she'd never be able to forgive herself, either.

So for now, she'd have to simply stem her own personal and professional curiosity and just let it go.

With her research and reporting skills, it wouldn't take her more than a day to put out enough feelers to find out anything she wanted about Lucas, but somehow that smacked of dishonesty.

And would indeed confirm his fears about reporter's snooping. Something she was determined never to stoop to.

If Lucas wanted her to know something, he'd tell her

once he trusted her enough, and that was the key—trust.

If he didn't tell her, or didn't want to tell her, she had no business digging into his personal life and background simply out of curiosity. He'd tell her what he wanted to know in his own good time, and until then she could wonder all she wanted—but she wasn't going to do anything about that wondering, at least for now.

Rubbing the tension gathered at the back of her neck, Katie walked to the credenza in her office and poured herself a cup of coffee, trying to clear her mind.

"Katherine?" Lindsey yelled from her desk and Katie almost winced, wishing Lindsey would just get up and walk to her office to talk to her.

"What?" she yelled back.

"Can I uh…ask you a personal question?"

Katie smiled. "Why not, everyone else in town does." She sighed. "My life is apparently an open book."

"When you were out this morning, did you by any chance get into more trouble?"

"Trouble?" Katie repeated, sipping her coffee. "No, why?"

"Because the police chief just pulled up in front of our office."

"That's impossible," Katie said, not even bothering to look. "The police chief is on a date with my mother." She wondered why the mere thought that Lucas would agree to a "date" with her mother tickled her to no end. She had to admit if the man thought her mother and her aunt were a bit strange he certainly didn't show it.

"No," Lindsey corrected. "The chief is coming through our front door."

Katie set her coffee down, almost sloshing it over the rim as she went to her office door. "Lucas, what are you doing here?" she asked with a concerned frown as he pushed through the front door, looking just a bit frazzled. "I thought you were having lunch with my mother."

"So did I," he said a bit sheepishly, nodding a greeting to Lindsey. "You haven't by any chance…uh…seen or heard from your mother, in the last hour or so have you?"

"No, why?" Katie asked suspiciously.

"Now, Katie I don't want you to get upset," Lucas said, crossing the office in two steps and gently lying his hands on her shoulders.

"That's exactly what Rusty says every time he has to tell me something that he *knows* is going to upset me. He says, 'now don't get upset, Ma, but' and then he tells me something that upsets me." Steeling herself, and trying not to panic, Katie took a deep breath. "Okay, I won't get upset," she lied, swallowing hard and looking up at Lucas as she laid her hands on his chest for additional support. Fear had a grip and he hadn't even told her what was wrong yet. "Just tell me, Lucas. Fast," she specified, clinging to his shirt. "Fast is always better," she said and he nodded.

"Katie, I'm sorry, but I think your mother's missing."

Chapter Six

"Missing," Katie repeated, not certain she fully understood and frowning as she tried to prevent full blown panic from getting a hold until she did. "Missing in that she forgot to meet you at the diner? Missing that she's late? Exactly what do you mean *missing, Lucas?*"

"She never made it to the diner, Katie," he said softly. "I got there about two minutes late, because I had to stop home and pick up one of the puppies. When I got there, I was afraid your mother had already been there and left, but Patience said she hadn't seen her all morning."

"She's probably with the mayor, I know they've been sparring lately, but—"

"Katie." The look on his face stopped her cold. "The mayor was having lunch with the fire chief when I got to the diner and Mayor Hannity said he hasn't seen your mother for almost two days." Lucas buried a smile. "Mayor Hannity says she's not speaking to him."

Katie nodded. Her mother stopped speaking to the mayor on average of once a week.

"She probably just forgot, Lucas," Katie said more for her own benefit than his. "She's probably at home still putting her makeup on—"

"Katie, I just came from your mother's house. No one's there. I checked everywhere I thought she could be. I went to the market, the beauty salon, the barbershop, the library and even the bank, but no one has seen your mother. I also went to the pharmacy, Dr. Robsen's office and I stopped by the new dentist's office." Lucas shook his head. "Katie, as far as I know, no one in town has seen her today."

Katie's heart went into double time as fear engulfed her. Suddenly cold, she wrapped her arms around her stomach. This was one of the things she'd feared most since her mother's stroke; that maybe one day Louella might simply forget who she was or where she was and just wander off.

In spite of Katie's fears, the doctor had told her she couldn't hover over her mother. She had to simply let Louella live her life and get back to her routine, which he promised in the end would help her mother recover her memory.

"Well, she doesn't drive anymore and the town is a full nine miles long. I doubt she could have walked out of town, so she has to be somewhere *in* town." Katie's voice was rising in spite of her resolve not to get upset.

"Katie, I think you're getting upset here," Lucas said,

lifting her chin so he could look into her eyes. She'd gone pale and her eyes were a bit glassy. Knowing how close she was to her mother and how worried she had to be tugged at something deep in his heart.

"Listen to me," he said quietly, but firmly. "I'm sure your mother's fine and there's probably a perfectly logical explanation—"

"Lucas," Katie all but moaned. "This is my mother we're talking about. No one's ever used the word logical and my mother in the same sentence before, and with good reason. Logic is really not her strong suit."

"Katie, I'm sure everything is fine. She's probably just running a bit late. Maybe she was delayed at her store—"

"The store." Katie brightened. "Aunt Gracie will know where my mother is. She never goes anywhere without telling Aunt Gracie." Katie didn't even bother to wait for his response, she simply headed toward the front door.

"You want to take my car?" Lucas asked, following right on her heels.

"No, we can walk to the Astrology Parlor just as quick as we can drive and at least we won't have to waste time parking."

"Katie, you want me to call your uncle at the cabin and tell him you've got an emergency and ask him to come in and handle the blue lines for you?" Lindsey asked, a concerned frown on her face.

"No!" Katie said, panic lacing her words as she raised both her hands in the air to stop Lindsey. The last thing she needed was to have to have her uncle come in and bail her out the first week she took over. That would hardly bode well for his confidence in her taking over the paper.

"No, thanks, Lindsey," Katie said, softening her voice and flashing the woman a strained smile. "I'll be right back and I promise I'll get those blue lines done and returned in plenty of time if I have to stay up all night to do them."

"Whatever you say," Lindsey said as Katie yanked open the door and strode through it with Lucas following her.

As she all but sprinted down the block, Katie's gaze scanned all the familiar stores and shops. But there was no sign of her mother.

"Lucas, what time were you supposed to meet my mother?"

"She said twelve-fifteen. I'll admit I was a few minutes late but when I got there, Patience said she hadn't seen or heard from her all day."

"Lucas, my mother is forgetful at times. Last year she had a slight stroke and it left her with short-term memory lapses, but she's never just up and disappeared before."

"Well we're not certain she's disappeared now, Katie. We've just…misplaced her at the moment," he said, reaching for Katie's hand as they hurried down Main Street.

At the Astrology Parlor, Katie peeked in the window, saw her Aunt Gracie, but no one else, and hurried in.

"Aunt Gracie? Have you seen Mama?"

Her aunt looked up from the tarot cards she'd been reading and smiled. Gracie Collier fit in the Astrology

Parlor like a part of the scenery. The entire parlor was decorated in comforting shades of misty blue, eggshell and silver. The ceiling was painted a dark blue with fake silver stars and an almost glowing full moon etched in silver and white against the blue backdrop. At night, a spotlight highlighted the moon so that from outside, it really looked like the moon was shining indoors.

Large silver astrological signs hung from the ceiling on wire and they twirled and whirled with every shift in the air. Comfortable, padded chairs also in shades of striped blue and eggshell lined the perimeter of the parlor, and two tables, one each for Louella and Gracie to work from, dominated the middle of the room. The plateglass window that fronted the parlor allowed the early afternoon sunlight to fill the room with sunny cheer.

"Hello, dear." Not one to be rushed, and always moving in her own good time, Gracie beamed and set her tarot cards down on the table. "You know if you would have called me I could have told you they were in the second box from the top in the row of boxes closest to the lamp."

Katie blinked at her aunt. "Excuse me?"

Gracie laughed. "Rusty's basketball shoes, sweetheart. You were looking for them this morning, weren't you?"

"Yes," Katie said. "I was." She rubbed her forehead where a headache had began clustering. "I'm sorry," she said with a smile, not wanting to alarm her aunt. "I didn't even think to call you. Next time I will."

"Good, dear. Now, what was it you asked?" Gracie inquired as she pushed up the sleeves of her flowing blue silk caftan. Before Katie could respond, her aunt's gaze shifted to Lucas, who was hovering behind Katie. "Good afternoon, Lucas," Gracie said with a big smile.

"Ma'am," Lucas returned with a smile of his own.

Gracie Collier was two years younger than her sister, but where Louella had ash blond hair, Gracie had let her hair go pure white. Cut short, it curled around her head in a riot of corkscrews that made her resemble an aging Shirley Temple. Still stunning at nearly seventy, with a sweet, childlike disposition, she wore little makeup except for bright red lipstick, and while Louella's clothes were more conservative, Gracie was known for her artful, silk caftans, most designed with stars, moons and other symbols of her life's work. She had them custom made at a shop in Madison and hadn't changed the style in almost forty years.

Katie moved closer and went down on one knee, taking her aunt's hands in hers. If she didn't capture Gracie's full attention, her aunt wouldn't be able to concentrate, and Katie knew from experience she'd never get any information from her. "Aunt Gracie?"

"Mmm, yes dear?" Gracie beamed down at her.

"Do you know where Mama is?"

"Why, of course dear. She's at the diner. She had a date. For lunch." Gracie smiled again. "She's at lunch with…Lucas," she said, her surprised gaze going from Katie to Lucas and back again. Her mouth went into a little O and she frowned slightly. "Lucas, have you and Louella finished your lunch already?"

"No, ma'am," he said, stepping closer. "Lady Louella never showed up."

"Well for goodness sake," Gracie said with a decided frown. "That can't be right. Are you sure, dear? Louella's never rude, and standing up a handsome man for a date is certainly rude in my book. I'll be sure to speak to her about it—"

"Aunt Gracie, she wasn't—" Katie hung her head and ground her teeth, fear nearly draining her patience. She had to stop to collect herself before she said something she shouldn't.

She'd learned a long time ago that when it came to her mother and aunt, they did and said things in their own good time, and no amount of nudging or rushing would hurry them along.

"Katie." Lucas took her gently by the shoulders and helped her up, sensing she was about at the end of her rope. "Let me try," he said softly, going down on his knee in front of Gracie so he would be eye level with her. "Miss Gracie," Lucas said with a smile, reaching for her hands the same way Katie had, "I was just wondering if you can think of anywhere, anywhere at all where Lady Louella might be right now?"

"Right now, dear?" Gracie repeated with a frown and Lucas nodded.

"Yes, right now."

"Well, let me think about it a moment." With that, Gracie closed her eyes, pressed her fingers to her lids, then leaned back against the chair, humming low and slow in her throat.

"Uh…Katie, what's she doing?" Lucas asked nervously, glancing over his shoulder.

"Thinking." Katie frowned, taking a step closer to him and putting a hand on his shoulder. "At least, I think she's thinking," Katie clarified.

She had to admit that Lucas was handling both her mother and aunt with a dignity and aplomb that most strangers, at least those not from Cooper's Cove, rarely possessed. And she had to admit it touched her deeply that in spite of how "different" her mom and aunt were, Lucas still treated them both with respect.

Although, considering they'd met when he caught *her* digging up his backyard in the middle of the night, she was probably in no position to talk about being "different."

"Well for goodness sake, why didn't Louella just tell someone?" Gracie asked as her eyes popped open and she smiled serenely. "I know where she is."

"Uh…where?" Lucas asked.

"The diner," Gracie announced in glee. "Arguing with Patience about having animals in the diner." Gracie frowned. "Although I didn't know the diner served animals, did you?"

"Miss Gracie? I…I uh…just came from the diner," Lucas said. "And Lady Louella wasn't there."

"Of course not, dear," Gracie said with a nod. "She was at the post office caught up in the lunch hour crowd. Then when she was walking to the diner, Mr. Hensen from the butcher's came out to talk to her. He took her inside to show her some pictures of his grandchildren back in Idaho, or Oklahoma, or some O state like that. That poor man," Gracie added with a shake of her head. "Ever since his wife died he has no one to talk to." Gracie brightened suddenly. "Lucas, I think you should give one to Lindsey and have her take it to Mr. Hensen. I think they'd enjoy each other."

"What?" Lucas asked, totally confused as he glanced back at Katie, whose face mirrored his. She shrugged at him before he turned back to Gracie.

"If you give one of the puppies to Lindsey and ask her to take it to Mr. Hensen, I think you'll find something very interesting develops between the three of them." Leaning forward, Gracie patted Lucas's hand. "I think the two of them are lonely, and would welcome the company and the companionship of someone else." She shrugged and chuckled. "And who knows what might develop between them."

"Uh…okay," Lucas said, realizing maybe this whole psychic-astrology stuff was a bit over his head.

Katie stepped forward as Lucas stood up. "Aunt Gracie, are you sure Mama's at the diner?"

"Why, I'm positive, sweetheart." Her eyes widened in dismay. "You don't think I'd lie to you, do you, Katherine?"

"Of course not," Katie said with a laugh, leaning over to kiss her aunt's cheeks. "I was just worried that's all."

"Well, sweetheart, no sense worrying. It never stopped or started anything from happening. You have a lot of stress right now, and it's not good for you to worry so much."

"May I use your phone, Miss Gracie?" Lucas asked. He'd given up his cell phone when he'd moved to Wisconsin since he didn't want to talk to anyone, especially reporters, all of whom seemed to have his cell phone on speed dial. He still hadn't dared replace it.

"Of course, dear. Of course." Gracie motioned him toward the phone and Lucas quickly dialed the diner as Gracie turned back to her niece. "And Katie, don't forget to congratulate your mother, dear."

"For what?" Katie asked in surprise.

"She's going to run for mayor."

"No, mama's *not* running for mayor, Aunt Gracie," Katie said firmly and Gracie's face shifted into confusion.

"Why dear, I could have sworn Louella told me she was running." She blinked at Katie. "Maybe I got it wrong?"

"No, Aunt Gracie, you didn't get it wrong. Mama just *thinks* she's running for mayor, but she's not. She's just saying that because she's mad at Mayor Hannity." A sudden thought occurred to Katie. "Aunt Gracie, do you have any idea why Mama's so angry with the mayor?"

Maybe if she could get to the bottom of her mother's anger—and she had no doubt it didn't have anything to do with the mayor canceling the seniors' potluck dinner—maybe, just maybe she could quash this wild idea her mother suddenly had to run for office.

Her aunt had the good grace to flush and look away. "Uh…I'm not certain, Katherine, dear." A faint smile curved her lips. "Perhaps you'd better ask your mother." Gracie patted her hand and leaned close to whisper. "It's a woman thing, dear, and I think it best if your mother told her yourself."

"A woman thing," Katie repeated, totally confused, and Gracie nodded.

"Yes, dear."

Okay, well then, she'd just add "talk to her mother about that woman thing" to the long, long list of things she had to do in the very near future.

Still on the phone, Lucas turned toward Katie and flashed a thumbs-up and a smile, then reached out and draped an arm around her shoulder as she nearly sagged in relief. Lucas drew her closer, kissing the top of her head as he continued to talk. He could feel the warmth of her soft curves as she all but sagged against him in relief, and he kissed her head again.

"Yes, Patience, she is? Good. No. Can you keep her there for me? Just tell her I'll be right there. And yes, I'll explain it's my fault you have a dog in the diner." He hung up the phone and grinned at Katie. "She's there and she's definitely fighting with Patience, but Patience is going to keep her there until I get there."

"Oh, thank goodness," Katie said, feeling a rush of relief. It was very hard to fight whatever was drawing her toward Lucas simply because he was so kind and she'd always been a sucker for kindness in a man.

Especially a gorgeous man.

Katie sighed, inhaling Lucas's male scent as she allowed herself to lean against him for a moment. It had been so long since she'd had *anyone* to lean on, especially when she was frightened or faced a crisis, that she'd forgotten how wonderful it was, knowing she wasn't alone, knowing there was someone right next to her, supporting and sharing her burden. Even if it was only for a few moments of a day, she was heartily grateful, especially since she didn't really need another crisis to handle today.

NO POSTAGE
NECESSARY
IF MAILED
IN THE
UNITED STATES

BUSINESS REPLY MAIL

FIRST-CLASS MAIL   PERMIT NO. 717-003   BUFFALO, NY

POSTAGE WILL BE PAID BY ADDRESSEE

SILHOUETTE READER SERVICE
3010 WALDEN AVE
PO BOX 1867
BUFFALO NY 14240-9952

Get FREE BOOKS and a FREE GIFT when you play the...

LAS VEGAS
GAME

Just scratch off the gold box with a coin. Then check below to see the gifts you get!

YES! I have scratched off the gold box. Please send me my **2 FREE BOOKS** and **gift for which I qualify.** I understand that I am under no obligation to purchase any books as explained on the back of this card.

335 SDL D7XM   235 SDL D7YN

FIRST NAME	LAST NAME

ADDRESS

APT.#	CITY

STATE/PROV.	ZIP/POSTAL CODE

(S-SE-10/05)

7	7	7	Worth TWO FREE BOOKS plus a BONUS Mystery Gift!
🍒	🍒	🍒	Worth TWO FREE BOOKS!
🔔	🔔	♣	TRY AGAIN!

www.eHarlequin.com

▼ DETACH AND MAIL CARD TODAY! ▼

"See, sweetheart, I told you." Gracie turned toward them with a smile.

"Miss Gracie, have you had lunch yet?" Lucas asked with a mischievous twinkle in his eye that had Gracie all but blushing.

"Lunch?" Coyly, Gracie patted her curls. "Well, dear, now that you mentioned it, I'm afraid I haven't."

"Well, I'd be honored if you'd join us for lunch."

"But…but what about Louella?"

Lucas grinned and held out his free arm for Gracie. "I'm sure she won't mind, after all it's not every day a man gets to escort two beautiful ladies to lunch." He glanced down at Katie, whom he still had his other arm around. "Unless you'd like to make it three beautiful women?"

Laughing at the compliment, Katie shook her head. "Thanks, Lucas, I appreciate it. But now that I know where my mother is and that she's safe, I've got to get back to work. I'm really pressed for time."

"All right." He hesitated. "And don't worry, I promise I'll keep an eye on your mother," he whispered so her aunt couldn't hear him.

"Thanks," she said in gratitude. "And I don't think you or Rusty need to worry about me getting home too early and spoiling his surprise. At this rate, if I'm home before eight it will be a miracle."

"Don't discount miracles," Gracie said, getting up and linking her arm through Lucas. "I've seen quite a few in my day." She patted the pearls around her neck. "Even caused a few, I might add."

Lucas looked at Katie, who shook her head. "Don't

even think about asking," she warned him. "Lucas…" Katie hesitated. "Thank you." She stood on tiptoe to kiss his cheek, making her aunt's eyes widen in delight. "I really appreciate everything you've done today."

"No problem," he said with a grin. "I'll see you and Rusty tonight, then?"

"Definitely." She leaned over and kissed her aunt's cheek. "Thanks, Aunt Gracie."

"You're very welcome, dear. I'll tell your mother you were looking for her."

"Thanks. Have a great lunch," Katie said as she dashed toward the door. Lucas and Gracie followed more slowly.

"Now, Lucas," Gracie began as they started down Main Street. "There's been something I've been meaning to tell you."

"Yes ma'am?"

"They've forgiven you, you know," she said quietly, turning to meet his startled gaze. His heart began to thud hard and heavy in his chest and he almost stumbled over his own two feet.

"Who?"

"Your family," Gracie said quietly, giving his arm a reassuring pat with her free hand as his face drained of color. "Your wife, Brenda, and your son, Todd. They forgave you a very long time ago, Lucas. Now don't you think it's time you forgave yourself, dear?"

Lucas turned to her, all but stopping in the middle of the sidewalk again. "Miss Gracie…how on earth did you know…" He let his voice trail off, not certain he really wanted to know.

Smiling serenely, she merely nudged him along.

"You know, dear, guilt intensifies our grief, allowing it to move through us like a syrup, spreading all through our system, covering our feelings and emotions and basically paralyzing them."

"But—"

"I know, dear, and it's only natural after what you've been through, but you aren't really living if you don't allow yourself to feel now, are you?"

He had to think about that for a moment, and realized perhaps for the first time he really wasn't living— just existing, going through the motions of life every day just wanting to get the day over with so he could be alone to savor and nurture his grief.

"I guess you're right," he admitted quietly.

"It's understandable, dear," she said with a smile. "But they've forgiven you, don't you think it's time for you to forgive yourself? It wasn't your fault, Lucas. Not at all. No one could have stopped or prevented what happened. Not even you, unless of course you've been granted divine powers?" she asked, her face ever hopeful as she looked up at him.

"Uh…no," he said firmly, shaking his head. "No divine power, no power at all as far as I can tell."

"A pity, really," she said with a sigh. "But no matter. There's no point in blaming yourself for something you couldn't stop or change, now is there?" She smiled. "You know, Lucas, they'd want you to be happy."

"I am happy," he insisted.

"You're not, dear. Not yet," she disagreed with a slow, charming smile. "But you will be, dear." She gave his arm another reassuring pat. "Soon. Very soon. I promise.

* * *

"Hey, Lucas?" Rusty said as he came bounding out the back door, letting it slam shut behind him. Dressed in ragged cutoffs, a faded T-shirt, sneakers and a Chicago Bears baseball cap that Lucas had given him earlier, he bolted down the back stairs two at a time.

"That was Ma on the phone." Rusty rolled his eyes as he jumped down the last two steps. "Again. Jeez, doesn't she know you can watch a kid like me without getting into trouble?" he asked with a frown.

Normally his grandma came and stayed with him after school. But today, she'd gone home when Lucas got here, and they'd spent all this time doing guy stuff— well, once they got all the boxes inside the house unpacked for his ma.

And his ma had called about a gazillion times checking on them—both of them. He shook his head. Jeez, he didn't know why his ma worried so much.

Lucas was really cool, and he'd kinda been wondering what it would be like to have someone cool like that for a dad. Since he never had a dad around all the time, at least not since he'd started school, it was hard to imagine having a father around all the time. Like Sean and all the other guys. Just thinking about it gave him a funny feeling in his stomach. He really liked Lucas, and Lucas had really neat ideas. Like about the clubhouse and stuff.

But Lucas had also talked to him about being a bit more responsible now that his ma was working so many hours trying to get settled in her new job. He'd never thought about the things he could do to make his ma's life easier. It wasn't something a guy thought of, but Lucas had.

He'd have never thought to unpack the boxes in the house since he didn't know what to do with the stuff when he got it unpacked. But Lucas had a cool system. They worked as a team and it went pretty fast. Lucas would unpack a box, and as he took out each item, Rusty would tell him which room the item went in. They'd just made big piles on the living room floor, and when the piles got big enough, they each took a pile, hauled everything to the right room and put it away. It wasn't so hard to figure out where to put the stuff when they did it that way.

"What did your mom say?" Lucas asked, glancing up from the swing he'd just finished hanging on the back porch. It was a housewarming present from Louella and Gracie. He'd taken them over to the hardware store this afternoon to pick it up, promising he'd hang it before Katie got home tonight.

"She's on her way home. Hey, that looks really cool," Rusty said with a grin, bounding over and giving the swing an experimental push. "My ma's gonna love it. That's all she ever talked about when we were in Madison, about how once we finally came home, we were going to buy a house, and she was going to buy a big old porch swing and just sit and swing and watch the world go by." He shrugged. "Don't know why anyone would wanna just sit," he said, scratching the side of his head. "Sounds boring to me, but hey, maybe when I get old like ma, maybe I'll just want to sit around and stare at nothing, too."

"You think so?" Lucas asked, trying to keep a straight face, and Rusty nodded.

"Yeah, maybe," he said with a frown, not sounding too sure. It had grown dark several hours ago, and they'd lit candles and a couple of tiki torches they'd found squirreled away in the garage, giving the yard a nice, amber glow. "Anyway, she's gonna freak when she sees it."

"And that's good?" Lucas asked with a lift of his brow.

"Awesome," Rusty assured him with a lightning flash grin.

"Awesome, huh?" Lucas repeated with a nod, pleased. He slung an arm companionably around Rusty's shoulder. He'd been both surprised and pleased at how easy it was to be around Rusty. He was a terrific kid, and just being with Rusty had, as he'd hoped, filled a small piece of that hole in his heart that he'd had ever since his own son's death. He'd forgotten how much fun being around a kid could be. "I'm very proud of you, Rusty."

"Me?" Stunned, Rusty's eyes widened and he shrugged, trying not to look too pleased. "How come?"

"Well, let's see, you helped unpack the entire house for your mother. You helped me hang the swing, you helped me put the grill together and you had that great idea about the picnic table." Lucas's gaze shifted to the backyard. "The table looks pretty awesome, too."

Rusty surveyed the makeshift picnic table that he and Lucas had put together from two sawhorses and an old door they'd found in the garage.

They'd set the table, put a bunch of candles down the middle for light, and then he'd run over to his grandmother's to borrow some flowers from her garden and stuck them in an empty olive oil bottle and set it on the table.

"Yeah, it does look pretty good," Rusty admitted, flushing with pride. "My ma's gonna be so surprised. She still thinks she's cooking when she gets home," he added with a grin.

Lucas glanced at his watch. "It's almost nine o'clock," he said with a slight frown. "It's a little late for her to be cooking after working all day, don't you think?"

Rusty shrugged. "Guess so." He'd never really thought about how many hours his ma worked. It was a lot, he suddenly realized, and then she worked when she got home, too. Jeez, didn't she ever get tired of working?

Lucas moved to the grill to check the coals he'd started almost half an hour ago. "I'm glad we decided to just bake some potatoes and grill a steak." Lucas tested the coals to see if they were hot enough to put the steak on. "You sure you don't want to eat?" Lucas asked, turning to Rusty, then adding with a grin, "Again?"

After unpacking the house, they'd walked into town and gotten a pizza for Rusty, since the kid swore he was starving, and he must have been since he all but inhaled the entire pizza. Lucas had forgotten how much boys this age could eat.

"Nah," Rusty said, rubbing his stomach. "I'm still stuffed from the pizza. I was kinda hoping to go in and start working on the sketches for the clubhouse."

"Sounds like a plan to me," Lucas said with a smile. "Once you show me what you've got in mind, I think we can get started on it right away."

"Really?" Excitement had Rusty nearly dancing in place.

"Yeah, really," Lucas confirmed with a smile. "You

said you had some ideas for some drawings, if you want to spend an hour or so before bed drawing something up, tomorrow after school and practice—"

"And chores and homework," Rusty added with a scowl.

"Yeah, and chores and homework. We can take a look at what your ideas are, see what kinds of material we'll need, and then talk to Jack at the lumberyard about the cost of the supplies."

"Costs?" Rusty said in a panic, his face falling. "I don't know how much this stuff costs." He mentally calculated his allowance this week with what was in his piggy bank. Although it wasn't a piggy, it was just a big old glass jar he used to save up for things. "I think I've got about eight dollars, including my allowance this week."

"Well, Rusty," Lucas said thoughtfully, "that reminds me of something I wanted to ask you. How would you and Sean and maybe a couple of your other friends like a temporary part-time job? Nothing to interfere with your schoolwork, nothing that would take too much time. It's sort of a community service job, for the town council," he specified vaguely. "It pays four dollars an hour for four hours on Saturdays for the next two Saturdays, after basketball practice of course."

"Four dollars a piece an hour for each of us?" Disbelief and delight streaked across Rusty's features.

"Yep."

Rusty mentally calculated how much money it would be and his eyes lit up. "Wow, that's almost a fortune."

"So you think you're interested?"

"Yeah, sure," Rusty said, trying not to show his excitement as he mentally counted up the cash again. "I could use the money for the clubhouse, and I'm sure Sean and some of the guys could use some extra money, too."

"Good. Good."

Rusty frowned. "So…uh…what do you—we have to do?"

"Well, how about if I tell you all about it once you ask Sean and some of your other friends. That way I can tell you all together. I figure we'll need about five boys in total."

"Okay," Rusty said with another shrug.

Lucas smiled. "Great." Lucas frowned as the coals shifted and sent up a spray of sparks from the grill. "If your mom's on her way home she should be here any minute. You want to run inside and get the steaks out of the fridge?"

"Yeah, sure." Rusty hesitated. "And I'll talk to Sean and a couple of the guys at school tomorrow about the job."

"Okay, do that. Thanks."

"Sure, and uh…Lucas?" Nervous now, Rusty was shifting from foot to foot, looking down at his tennis shoes.

Lucas turned back to Rusty and found himself smiling. "Yes, son."

Rusty dared a glance at him. "Uh…Lucas, thanks. For…uh…everything today."

"You're welcome, Rusty. You're very welcome," Lucas said.

"So I'm…uh…gonna see you…tomorrow?" Rusty asked.

"Definitely. We're going to practice some hoops,

right? Work on your passing and blocking? And go over the clubhouse plans."

Relieved, Rusty grinned. "Cool. If you don't mind, after I get the steaks for you, I'm gonna go work on the clubhouse drawings."

"Oh, and Rusty," Lucas said, stopping the boy in his tracks as he turned on his heel to bolt toward the house. Rusty looked at Lucas over his shoulder.

"Yeah?"

"Thank you," Lucas said softly and Rusty flashed him a big, crooked grin.

"No sweat." Rusty bolted toward the house, leaving Lucas with a surprisingly warm feeling wrapped around his heart.

By the time Katie pulled into her driveway it was almost 9:00 p.m. and she was utterly exhausted and famished. But she'd gotten the blue lines done and sent to the printer, stopped at Mr. Hensen's to pick up her meat, and gone to the market to get some bare necessities like potatoes, napkins and ketchup for dinner, before finally heading home.

After gathering her groceries and the pile of edits she'd brought home with her, she slid out of the car and locked it. She'd almost forgotten about Rusty's surprise until she saw the soft flickering of lights in the backyard.

In spite of her fatigue, she smiled to herself. It was so strange to be coming home, knowing someone was waiting for her. It was a luxury she'd never had before and awakened something deep inside of her.

As she rounded the yard, her heart tumbled as she

took everything in—the makeshift picnic table, the candles flickering on the set table, and Lucas, dressed casually in jeans and a shirt with the sleeves rolled up, standing over the grill. It was such a homey scene, one that was probably played out across thousands of households every evening, but never in *her* household.

Until now.

"Lucas?" She had a hard time talking around the lump in her throat. Seeing him here, in this homey atmosphere, *her* home specifically, did something to that yearning deep in her heart, the one that had been aching a little bit harder ever since she'd laid eyes on Lucas. She was just tired, she assured herself, trying to ignore the emotions clogging her throat.

"Hi, you finally made it," he said, turning to her with a smile. "You look beat," he added with concern, seeing the smudge lines of fatigue under her eyes and the weary slump of her shoulders.

She sniffed the air and almost swooned. "Is that food I smell?" Her empty stomach groaned. Grilled meat mixed with the crisp scent of fall had her mouth watering.

He grinned. "It is. Hope you don't mind—"

"Mind?" She shook her head, pressed a hand to her ravenous stomach and quelled the urge to throw her arms around him in gratitude. "I haven't eaten a morsel all day and I'm starving." Guilt quickly set in and she moved closer. "Lucas, I'm sorry, I was supposed to make you dinner, remember?"

In spite of the guilt, she had to admit it was a relief to know she didn't have to cook dinner right now. She was dead-tired and the idea of just being able to sit down and eat something someone else had cooked seemed like an incredibly indulgent luxury.

"After the day you've had, Rusty and I figured you could use a break. I've got potatoes baking and almost done." Glancing at his watch, he said, "And the steak should be done by the time you get changed into something more comfortable."

She laughed. "You know, I've heard that line a hundred times in the movies, but I never thought I'd actually have someone say it to me. Where's Rusty?" she asked, glancing around.

"In his room working on the drawings for the clubhouse. He did his chores and his homework, and we went into town and got a pizza for him earlier."

She laughed. "I'm sure that was a real hardship for him," she said, knowing how much her son loved pizza. "Oh, I stopped by the butcher on my way home." Her lips twitched. "Seems Lindsey was at Mr. Hensen's. Said she'd brought Mr. Hensen a puppy. Said it was your idea. That you asked if she could take one over to him." Her lips were twitching again, knowing Lucas was playing matchmaker at the behest of her Aunt Gracie. "The two of them, or rather the three of them including the puppy, seemed to be having a fine time."

Lucas grinned. "Is that so? Well, I'll be." He shook his head, realizing maybe there was something to Gracie's psychic abilities. "But I can't take credit for it. It was your Aunt Gracie's idea, remember? I told Patience and Lindsey that they could have the puppies for a few hours, just to sort of get acquainted, but then they'd have to return them to their mom for a few more weeks until they're ready to be weaned. The fire chief's taking one and I've almost got the mayor convinced he needs a dog as well, so that means I only have one left to find a home for. And the mama, of course." He frowned a bit. "Although I really hate to separate Bert and Ernie."

"Bert and Ernie?" Katie repeated with a laugh and he nodded.

"I named the mama Bertrice, and the puppy Ernie, so they're Bert and Ernie, get it?"

She laughed again. "Seems to me you're rather attached to both of them."

"I am," Lucas admitted with a sigh. "Something about helping a lady in distress, I guess. I may have to keep both of them," he decided, wondering what on earth he was going to do with two dogs. But he thought they would help keep the loneliness at bay, especially at night when his own personal demons seemed to create havoc with his mind and his memories.

Trying to put both out of his mind, Lucas checked the steak, closed the grill, then crossed to Katie, taking her things out of her arms, and reaching for her hand. "Would you like to see Rusty's surprise?"

She laughed. "You mean dinner isn't it?"

"Nah, not a chance." He led her toward the back porch. She came to a halt, her vision swimming when she saw the swing. "Oh Lucas…" Her voice trailed off and she blinked away her tears, touched so deeply she could barely speak. "You… You…" She had to swallow before continuing. "You have no idea…"

He laughed. "Oh, yes, I do—Rusty told me all about

it. Complete with a roll of the eyes, a shoulder shrug and the notion that maybe when he got old like you, maybe he'd want to just sit and swing and stare at nothing, too."

She laughed, but wiped her eyes.

"Hey," he suddenly said in alarm. "You're not crying are you?" He studied her, trying not to panic.

"Me?" She scoffed, but wiped her eyes again and sniffled. "Not a chance." But the lump that had clogged her throat had moved somewhere near her heart, making it ache.

"Lucas, thank you—"

"Oh, no, don't thank me," he said, giving her hand a squeeze. "Thank your mother and your aunt. It's their housewarming gift to you. I was just the handyman who hung it."

Her gaze met his. "So I take it this isn't Rusty's surprise, either?"

"Nope."

She patted her heart as Lucas led her up the back stairs. "I don't know if my *old* heart can take all this excitement at one time," she teased.

When he led her inside the kitchen, her eyes widened when she saw that all the boxes that had been in the kitchen were gone. "Lucas, where is everything?" She looked up at him and he grinned.

"Where it's supposed to be. I hope," he added with a chuckle, leading her into the dining room and then the living room. "I can't guarantee it, but we did our best."

She stared, slowing turning around in a circle. When she left this morning, the entire house could have been declared a disaster area. Boxes, some half-full, some still full were scattered in every room of the entire house.

Now, there wasn't a box in sight.

"You—"

"No," Lucas said carefully. "Rusty unpacked the boxes and put everything away. Me, I just helped," he said, refusing to take credit.

Katie whirled in a circle again. She knew her son. Knew he'd never have done anything like this without a little prodding. He was a good kid, and very thoughtful—when he thought about it—but he was still a *kid,* and the idea of unpacking the house for her wouldn't have occurred to him without a little encouragement.

"Well." Katie patted her thudding heart again. "I guess this entire evening has been a surprise. I...I don't know what to say or how to thank you, Lucas." Needless to say, her concerns about Lucas being involved with her son because she knew so little about him were quickly evaporating.

"You're entirely welcome, but it's really Rusty you should thank. And your mom and aunt." He dumped all her stuff on the dining room table. "Why don't you do that and then change into something comfortable while I go check on the steaks?"

Still too moved to speak, she merely nodded as he headed toward the back door and let himself out.

Katie stood there for a moment, glancing around in utter surprise before leaning against the door and saying a silent prayer for her yearning heart.

Because she was terribly afraid that in spite of her very best efforts, her feelings for Lucas were suddenly strong, real and not at all brotherly.

Chapter Seven

As September raced along and fall settled in, the days grew shorter and cooler, and Katie's life seemed to take on a familiar and comfortable pattern.

With Lucas and Rusty totally involved in building the clubhouse, most nights when she got home Lucas was still there, and invariably, the three of them would have dinner together. Either she cooked when she got home, or Lucas had something wonderful sizzling on the grill, or they walked into town for pizza or went to the diner for dinner, but whatever they did, they seemed to do together.

If Katie worried about her growing feelings, she continually told herself Lucas's interest was primarily in her son, and she had to admit, Rusty seemed to be blossoming under Lucas's patient, tender care. She wasn't going to ruin something so wonderful for her son simply because she couldn't keep a firm grip on her own feelings.

She was finally getting a handle on her duties at the paper, and gaining a measure of true confidence, but there were still days when an emergency cropped up, or an ad was late, or something else unexpected popped up and she didn't get home until late, and Lucas always volunteered to stay with Rusty until she did get home.

It seemed as if her mom and aunt were unusually busy—although Katie could have sworn her mother was deliberately avoiding her—since talk of her mother's mayoral candidacy was still being whispered about all over town, much to Katie's chagrin.

Katie had a feeling her mother didn't want to discuss her sudden political ambitions with her, and she couldn't figure out why. Something was definitely up with her mother, but she hadn't had enough time to actually sit down with her mom and get to the bottom of what her aunt described as "a woman's thing." And every time she'd tried, her mother had made some excuse or canceled at the last minute, leaving Katie with lots of questions and no answers. Certain nothing was seriously wrong, Katie realized if it had waited this long, a little bit longer wouldn't hurt anything.

Traditionally in the Midwest, the last weekend in October marked a distinct change in the weather from balmy fall to chilly, wet pre-winter weather. But this year, the change came early, catching Katie off guard. By the end of the first week in October, the weather had already turned, dropping temperatures into the mid-forties and bringing buckets of rain that seemed to make the days dark, damp and dreary.

Trees shed their leaves completely, blowing barren limbs in the brisk wind as the town became totally involved in planning the Halloween festival, which would take place the last weekend of the month.

With all the extra newspaper coverage for the festival, Katie found herself working longer hours once again. Normally, Lindsey would be helping her, but this year Lindsey seemed unusually busy with her own activities and Katie found herself taking on more and more of the work. But she didn't mind.

Lindsey had put in her fair share of overtime over the years, getting out annual special editions without ever complaining about the extra hours or work, so Katie figured the woman was due a break.

Although Lucas and Rusty still talked about going up to Lucas's cabin for a weekend, Katie knew she wasn't going to be able to get away for a whole weekend until after the Halloween festival, not with so much work facing her.

As the colder weather set in, Lucas and Rusty raced to finish the clubhouse, wanting to get most of the work done before the worst of winter and snow set in.

On a Thursday evening near the end of the second week in October, Katie was just packing up her stuff to leave the office when the phone rang.

"*Cooper's Cove Carrier,* Katie speaking."

"Ma, when you coming home?"

She laughed. "Well, hi, honey, it's nice to talk to you, too."

"Ma," Rusty complained on a whine. "Come on."

"I was just leaving, honey," she said, shoving the sheaf of ads for the Halloween issue into her briefcase. "Why?" she asked, suddenly alarmed. "Is something wrong?"

He giggled. "Lucas said you would say that. You were right, Lucas," she heard her son yell. Hearing how easily the camaraderie had developed between Rusty and Lucas always made her smile.

"Okay, smart guy, what's up?" she asked with a laugh.

"We got a surprise for you. When you get home. So when are you coming home?"

"As soon as I hang up I'm heading out the door." She hesitated. "Does this surprise involve anything gross?" she asked, always wanting to be on the safe side. With an adolescent boy, she never knew.

Rusty giggled. "Nah, Ma, nothing gross. So hurry up and come home, will you?"

She could hear the excitement in his voice and smiled. "I'm on my way, sweetheart."

"Oh, and Ma, Lucas said not to worry about dinner. We're going out to celebrate and then is it okay if Lucas comes back here so we can watch the Bulls game tonight? They're playing the Cavs and we wanna see LeBron James."

"Who?" she asked with a frown, then shook her head. "Never mind. Of course it's okay, honey." Lucas had seamlessly fit into their lives as if he belonged there. It had happened too quickly and too easily for her to have given it a moment of concern. "So we're celebrating, huh? I suppose you don't want to give me a hint what we're celebrating, do you?"

"Nah, it's a surprise. It'll be better if you see for yourself."

"Okay, sweetheart. I'm on my way." Katie hung up the phone, finished packing her gear and headed out to her car, shivering as the brisk and slightly bitter wind gleefully whipped around her, wondering what kind of surprise Rusty and Lucas had conjured up for her this time.

"Rusty, if you don't stop tugging on your mother's arm like that, you're going to tug it right out of the socket," Lucas said with a laugh, rescuing Katie's hand from her son to enfold it in his own.

"But she's walking so slow," Rusty complained, dancing backward down the sidewalk that led around his house as Lucas and his mother followed.

"That's because I'm old, remember?" Katie quipped, making her son grin.

"Yeah, that's right. I forgot." Rusty sighed impatiently, sneaking a glance at his mother and Lucas holding hands. It was nice, he thought. Real nice. He was pretty sure Lucas liked him, but he really wanted Lucas to like his ma, too.

He caught them kissing once, when they thought he was in bed. He *had* been in bed, but he'd gotten thirsty and got up to get a drink. Lucas was leaving and Katie was standing in the doorway, talking to him. Then Rusty saw Lucas slip his arms around his ma's waist and pull her close. Then Lucas pressed his lips against his mother's. Rusty had never seen a man kiss his ma before, and for a minute he was shocked. Then he realized that other kids' moms and dads probably kissed a lot.

It was then he decided that maybe Lucas liked him *and* his mom. He sure hoped so. Thinking about it had given him that funny feeling in his stomach again.

He'd slipped back to bed before they saw him, but then he couldn't go to sleep because he just kept thinking again what it would be like to have Lucas for a dad.

And he realized then if that was ever gonna happen, Lucas had to like both *him and his ma.*

The thought scared him since he didn't even know if his ma liked Lucas, or any other man, since they'd never had a man around them. Not when they lived with his grandmother, not even when they lived in Madison. Never.

In a way, Lucas was kind of like a dad, he'd reasoned, since they did a lot of things together. And Lucas taught him things, helped him with his homework, especially his math and science, which he hated, and Lucas also taught him about sports.

But Rusty wanted a *real* dad, like Sean's and Kevin's, and Bobby's. Their dads lived in the same house, and ate dinner with them every night and were there every morning when they got up and were even there on weekends and holidays, too.

He wanted that, too, he realized. A lot. A *real* lot. More than anything. But had no idea how to make it happen.

Yet.

"Hey Ma, stop there," Rusty said, holding out his

hands to make sure she did. They'd turned on the garage lights and the backyard lights so that they were all highlighted against the dark night.

"Can I open my eyes now?"

"Yeah, you can open your eyes," Rusty said proudly.

Katie blinked. "Oh, my goodness, you finished the clubhouse." She took a step closer to get a better look. It was almost a perfect square built out of wood that had been stained a beautiful oak color, with a tall, narrow front door, windows cut out of the wood on either side of the door, and a rope ladder leading up the front of the structure.

"It's beautiful," she murmured, glancing at Lucas, who seemed to be grinning as proudly as her son.

"Me and Lucas finished it this afternoon," Rusty said, all but dancing in place he was so excited. "And look at this," he said, bounding over to the rope stairs that unfolded from the clubhouse and giving them a shake. "See these stairs? Once me and the guys are up there and inside, we can pull the stairs up so no girls can bother us."

"Girls? Or mothers?" Katie asked with a lift of her brow, earning a roll of her son's eyes.

"Ma, come on. You wanna come up and see inside? It's really cool. Lucas and I put in a real floor. We had to measure the boards so they'd be exact and I think I screwed up a few, but Lucas said it wasn't that important, that we'd make it work." His grin flashed. "And we did. Lucas has some old pillows and cushions he said we could have so we'd have something to sit on. And I'm gonna put some of my stuff up there, too. So what do you think, huh?"

"Rusty, it's a beautiful clubhouse and I'm very, very proud of you." She reached out to ruffle his hair, knowing he'd flinch and moan if she tried to kiss him in front of Lucas.

"So do you want to come up now, huh?" He was all but bouncing out of his tennis shoes as he held out the rope stairs to her.

"Uh…honey, there's something I've been meaning to…uh…tell you," Katie stammered, glancing helplessly from her son to Lucas.

"Jeez," Rusty complained. "Do you have to tell me *now?* Can't you just tell me…like after we go up and see the clubhouse."

Lucas was watching Katie and immediately something struck him. He gave her hand an affectionate squeeze. "Now, Rusty, forgive me for bringing this up, but I seem to recall the first day we talked about building the clubhouse, you specifically stated no girls allowed, remember?"

"Yeah, but, she's not a girl," Rusty protested, with a frown. "She's just my mom."

Katie laughed. "Yeah, I am, *just your mom,* kid, and I hate to break this to you, but I'm also one of those dreaded girls," she said, making a face at him with the last two words, which made him grin. She had a feeling his attitude toward girls would change in about a year or two. She wasn't quite certain how she felt about that, and preferred not to think about it until the time came.

"And you did say no girls," Lucas reminded him.

"Yeah, but then how's she gonna see inside?" Rusty asked with a scowl, scratching his cheek.

"Pictures," Katie said, inspired. "You and Lucas can take some pictures of the inside and that way I won't be breaking your clubhouse code."

"A clubhouse code," Rusty repeated, his face brightening as he decided he liked the idea. "Cool." He was back to bouncing on his heels again. "Hey, Lucas, could we maybe make a sign and list the clubhouse code, too? We could put all the rules on it and stuff."

"Sure thing," Lucas agreed easily, earning a grateful smile from Katie.

"Uh…Ma? There's something else," Rusty said. "Tomorrow's Friday, and we don't got school on Saturday."

"No school? I'll have to speak to someone about that," she said, shaking her head.

He grinned, as she'd expected. "Well, do you…uh… remember what you promised? That when we finished the clubhouse I could have the guys over for a sleepover. In the clubhouse? Do you remember, huh? And since tomorrow's Friday—"

"And you don't have school on Saturday," she finished for him with a nod, getting the picture.

"Yeah, right, so I was kinda wondering, could I maybe have my sleepover tomorrow night?" Eyes wide and hopeful, he stood there holding his breath, trying not to fidget.

"Well, Rusty, you know what I always say."

His face fell. "Aw, Ma, come on, you don't expect me to remember everything you always say, do you?" he asked.

She laughed. "This time I do. I've always told you a

promise is a promise, and since I promised, well…" She shrugged and smiled at him. "I guess we're having a sleepover tomorrow."

Excitement trumped worrying about looking cool and he yelled and jumped, high-fiving the air. "Awesome. And could we have pizza and soda, and would you maybe make some popcorn? Not the microwave kind, but the kind grandma makes in a skillet with real butter and salt and stuff?" The words were spilling out of his mouth faster than fizz in a shaken soda.

"Yes, pizza and soda and popcorn and stuff. As much stuff as you can eat," she promised with a laugh, her fatigue fading under her son's joy.

Enjoying himself, Lucas decided to enter the fray. "Rusty, if you want, I've got a battery-operated television with a VCR. If you want to rent some movies, you guys can watch the movies tomorrow night up in the clubhouse."

"Really?" Bursting with excitement, Rusty all but danced around Lucas and his mother. "Awesome." He grinned. "Can we get real spooky movies since it's almost Halloween?"

"You know the rules, kid," Katie cautioned. "No slasher movies. No movies with knives, guns or decapitation."

His face fell, but brightened suddenly. "What about some of those really old Creature Features we used to watch together. You know, the ones that don't got any color, and have that funny looking guy who wore that black cape all the time and thought he was a bat or something?"

"You mean Count Dracula with Boris Karloff?"

"Yeah, yeah, that's the one. Can we get some of those, Ma, huh? They're kinda cool."

Considering they were more campy than scary, Katie nodded her head. "Fine, but I get final approval on all movies. Deal?"

"Deal," he said. "Wait until I tell the guys. Can I go call Sean and everybody right now?"

"Go ahead," Katie said with a laugh, enjoying her son's excitement. "If any of the mothers want to talk to me, let me know. But make sure you tell them I'll be here supervising all night long."

"Yeah, and if you don't mind, I'll be your backup," Lucas said, knowing how rambunctious a group of preteen boys could be when they were together, and all wound up. "Reinforcements never hurt the cause," Lucas added knowingly.

"You'll come, too?" Rusty asked, his eyes widening hopefully, and Lucas looked at Katie.

"If it's all right with your mom. After all I've got to bring the television over anyway."

"That would be wonderful," Katie admitted, realizing Lucas knew of her fear and was trying to cover for her. "And since you've done all of this, and are supplying the television, how about if I make dinner? A sort of thank-you dinner," she added softly. Their gazes met and clung.

Katie's stomach tumbled over, as it always did whenever Lucas looked at her like that. It made her feel as if she was the only woman in the world.

Unabashedly pleased, Lucas grinned. "You've got

yourself a date." He froze the moment the words were out, realizing what he'd said, but to his relief, Katie didn't seem to notice.

"But we're having pizza, right?" Rusty asked, just wanting to be sure.

"Yes. As much as you can eat," Katie assured him. "Now go call your friends so we can have dinner."

Watching her son lope off, Katie laughed and shook her head, aware that Lucas was still holding her hand, his fingers warm and comforting on hers.

"How on earth did you know?" she asked the moment Rusty was out of earshot.

"What? That you were afraid of heights?" he asked with a laugh when she nodded and pressed her hand to her stomach. Just talking about heights made her queasy. "Probably because you lost about three shades of color from your face when Rusty asked you if you wanted to go up."

"If I was meant to be that high up in the air, I'd have been born with a parachute," she said with a scowl, only mildly embarrassed by her fear. "Or wings."

"Yeah, well, we've all got our little secrets," he said with a chuckle, nudging her around to start toward the house.

Yes, we do, she thought, but decided not to say anything, not wanting to spoil the wonderful mood. But Lucas's secrets were still preying on her mind. As much as she'd tried to put them aside, it was hard to ignore the fact that he still didn't trust her enough to tell her about his past. However, she simply couldn't bring herself to ask him about his past, not again.

At least not yet. Now wasn't the time, she realized. Not tonight when her son was so filled with joy. She couldn't remember when she'd seen Rusty so happy.

And she knew she had Lucas to thank. Oh, the things this man was doing to her heart, she mused silently.

"Lucas?"

"Mmm?" he asked as they started up the back steps.

"I don't know how to thank you. You've done so much for Rusty, made such a difference in his life. Maybe I wasn't exactly thrilled with this idea at first, I mean I didn't know enough about the Buddy for a Boy program to feel all that comfortable, but you've made me very comfortable. And my son very, very happy." And for that she would be forever grateful.

"He's made me happy, too, Katie," he said softly, turning to her. They hadn't bothered with the back-porch light and now they stood bathed in the soft darkness of early evening. The wind blew up, and Katie shivered. "I can't tell you how much being with Rusty has meant to me, too," he added.

And he knew he couldn't tell her, couldn't tell her about the heartbreak and pain that had been such a part of his life for so long he almost couldn't remember when it hadn't been a part of him.

He couldn't tell her how just being around her and Rusty had somehow miraculously seemed to lighten his grief. It hadn't erased it, nothing ever would, but for the first time in two years he began to feel as if there truly was some light at the end of this long, dark tunnel of pain.

"Rusty's truly an exceptional kid," he added, slipping

his arms around her to bring her closer when he saw her shiver again. "You should be very proud of him." He hesitated. "Cold?"

"A little," she said softly, lifting her chin to look at him. He took a step closer as he drew her nearer to him until their bodies were only a breath apart.

His eyes were so blue, so beautiful, so pained. It always made her own heart ache a little to see such pain and sadness in Lucas's eyes. What kind of pain, what kind of grief put that look in his eyes?

She wasn't certain she could answer that question.

His eyes were telling her there still wasn't the kind of trust of her—in her—that should be there, especially now that he'd gotten to know her, her son and her family so well, but his body was saying something entirely different.

His eyes might deny wanting her, or feeling anything for her, but his body—warm, masculine and pressed against hers—was telling her something else.

For tonight, she was simply going to enjoy the evening. And let her heart lead her. Just for tonight.

"Katie, thank you for sharing your son with me." Overcome by all the emotions swarming him, Lucas leaned in and gently brushed his lips against hers.

She moaned softly, lifting her hands to his shirt, then sliding them up to his neck, hanging on as he deepened the kiss until she felt as if the ground had tilted under her.

Awakened on some deep, primal level, she moaned and leaned into him, giving back as much as he gave, forgetting about all her rules and obligations for a moment to savor this.

Her arms tightened around him as his tongue gently outlined her lips, plunging her into a kaleidoscope of feelings that swirled through her, threatening to drown her in a sea of emotions so strong, so intense, she could feel her entire world shift off balance.

She loved the scent of him, the touch of him, the feel of him, and now, she simply let herself enjoy it. Gave herself permission to forget everything and just savor every delicious moment.

For the first time in a long time she no longer felt like just an overworked single mom, or a doting daughter, or a responsible reporter. She felt like a young, vibrant woman with wants and needs.

And desires. Desires that she'd buried and kept banked for as long as she could remember.

But now, Lucas had awakened in her all the things she'd been trying to deny for so very long. Knowing he'd awakened such feelings frightened her, but not enough to pull out of his arms.

Joy. It had been so long since she'd felt it, she almost didn't recognize it, that wild flight of all thought, all reason, escaping quickly so that a lightness and peace, a wild contentment, could seep into all the places that reason and thought had once filled.

Something dark and dangerous kindled, then leapt to life inside Lucas, something he'd carefully kept contained and controlled for over two years. But now, touching Katie, kissing her, just being with her had awakened so many sleeping demons, demons he wasn't certain he'd be able to control.

There was something between them, something so

primal and urgent, he felt it rip through him wildly, sending his every nerve ending on a roller-coaster ride.

Slowly, degree by degree, he deepened the kiss, dragging Katie even closer until she was pressed against the length of him. The softness of her body, the pliancy of her trust, touched his heart in a way that astounded him.

Lust. He remembered it sneaking up on him the night he met her, remembered, too, the guilt that came with it—guilt that he could still feel such a normal, human emotion when he'd been all but certain every emotion he'd ever had had withered and died on a cold Chicago morning two years ago.

Trying to catch his breath, and regain some control, Lucas tightened his hands on Katie's slender waist and reluctantly drew back from her.

Her eyes were dreamy and unfocused, her lower lip slightly puffy and red from his mouth.

How could he ever explain to her that he couldn't allow himself to feel anything for her? Couldn't allow himself to open up or trust anyone that much again?

He needed to step back, put some distance between them until he was certain he could control himself and his emotions. Something he'd never had a problem with until he'd met Katie.

"Look, Katie, I think—"

"Hey, Ma?" Rusty appeared in the doorway, and Katie flushed, not certain how long her son had been standing there or how much he'd seen. Self-consciously, she eased back a bit from Lucas.

"Yes, honey?" she said, turning to him with a smile.

He didn't look traumatized or alarmed, merely impatient, so she tried to relax.

"Sean's ma wants to talk to you about tomorrow night."

"Okay, honey, I'll be right in." She turned to Lucas, dragged a hand through her hair and blew out a breath, trying to garner back some control. "Sorry," she said with a shrug and a smile. "Duty calls."

Nodding, he opened the door for her, wondering exactly what he was going to do about his growing feelings for her. And her son. Feelings he knew in his heart were forbidden if he wanted to protect himself.

You could really learn a lot about a woman watching how she handled a houseful of rowdy, rambunctious preteen boys, Lucas realized the next evening.

Leaning against the counter in Katie's kitchen as she all but had to shovel from the kitchen table the debris the boys had left behind from dinner, Lucas watched her and marveled.

"Well, I'd say you've done this more than once before," he said mildly, a smile playing along his lips.

"Which part?" she asked with a laugh, as she continued to shovel paper goods, napkins, plates and cups into the garbage bag she was holding. "The part when they started tossing pizza back and forth at each other. Or when they decided to have a burping contest and guzzled down almost two quarts of soda in about five minutes flat?"

"Actually, I think my personal favorite was when they decided to have a spitting contest to see who could spit soda the farthest," he said mildly, tucking his tongue in his cheek to try to contain a smile.

"Well, with four brothers of your own I'm sure this brought back lots of memories," she said, glancing up at him and watching him nod as he tried to bank a smile.

"Oh, yeah. Like I said, my brothers and I gave my mom our fair share of trouble."

"Trouble," Katie repeated with a nod. "Now that's a word that goes pretty much hand in hand with raising boys. That and the phrase, 'What on earth were you thinking?'" she said with another laugh. "I'll bet every mother of a boy has said that phrase about a million times."

"At which point most boys answer, 'Thinking? What do you mean what was I thinking, Ma?'" Lucas supplied, laughing and remembering his own son's frequent refrain. "'I wasn't…thinking.'"

"Exactly." Katie realized he knew a lot more about raising boys than he'd ever let on. Much more, she had a feeling, than just being one of four boys in a family would allow. It was interesting and curious, she decided, and just added to her growing list of questions about Lucas's past.

"But all in all I think you handled everything well," he commented, glancing out the kitchen window to make sure the boys were still in the clubhouse. He'd personally supervised them going in and up, making certain they were safe and sound before admonishing them they were not to come down, leave, or go anywhere without letting him or Katie know. "You managed to hang onto your temper, your patience, and your sanity—no small feat I might add."

Pleased in spite of herself, Katie shrugged off his

compliment. "I've had lots of experience," she said, as she swiped the last of the debris off the table and closed and tied up the garbage bag. "I never intended for Rusty to be an only child," she said quietly, glancing up at him. "I guess maybe because I was an only child, I wanted him to have the experience of having brothers and sisters." She shrugged again, but he could hear the wistfulness in her voice. "But I guess it wasn't destined in my life plan," she said easily, trying to hide the disappointment as she set the garbage bag by the door to be taken out. "So I've always tried to make certain Rusty had plenty of friends to make up for it. He and Sean have been friends since first grade. Come to think of it, Rusty's probably known all the boys for that long and I've always encouraged Rusty to bring his friends home."

"If he's here, you don't have to worry about what he's doing."

"Exactly," she said, realizing he knew more than a thing or two about raising kids, boys specifically, that had nothing to do with having brothers.

"That's what my mother always said," he confessed with a smile. "Even with five boys of her own she still encouraged us to have our friends over. There probably wasn't a weekend when we didn't have at least two or three extra kids bunking down at our house."

"Sounds like you had a very wonderful childhood."

"Yeah," he admitted softly. "I did. We weren't rich by any means. I mean my dad was a cop and on a cop's salary raising five kids wasn't easy, but we never went without and we always knew there was an abundance of love, even if there wasn't always an abundance of material things." He hesitated. "It's hard for me to imagine being an only child." He didn't think any kid should be an only child, which is why he'd wanted more children so badly.

Katie nodded, absorbing everything he said, desperately trying to put the few pieces of this puzzle called Lucas Porter together.

"I think when you have an only child it's just common sense to want your kid to have plenty of close friends to sort of make up for being alone all the time," she admitted.

"So you wanted more kids?" he asked quietly, dampening a sponge from the sink and handing it to her.

"Oh, yeah," she admitted as she wiped down the kitchen table. "I actually wanted a houseful."

"But what about your career?" Lucas asked carefully.

Katie stopped wiping and looked up at him. "What about it?" Cocking her head, she studied him. "Please don't tell me you're one of those men who doesn't believe a woman can have kids *and* a career?" She was going to throw the sponge at him if he was, she thought, as the phone rang. "Excuse me," she said, scooting around the table to snatch up the phone.

"Hello?" She smiled, tucking the phone between her ear and shoulder so she could wipe down the counter. "Hi Mama, yes, the boys are having a ball. Copious amounts of pizza and soda for dinner, along with a couple of spitting contests and the like. Now I'm just cleaning up and getting ready to make them a few barrels of popcorn. Tomorrow?" Katie frowned. "Oh, yeah, right, the seniors' dance. No, no, I didn't forget," she lied, rolling her eyes because she had forgotten it. "Yes, I'm still covering it for the paper since Lindsey's unavailable. Yes, I'll make sure I'm there by 5:30 tomorrow. Okay, Mama. Oh, and maybe we'll have a chance to talk," Katie said hopefully, then stopped. "You want to talk to me, too?"

Well now that was a switch, Katie thought in amusement, considering her mother had been avoiding talking to her at any length about anything important— deliberately, she was certain—for the past few weeks.

"Okay, Mama, I'll see you tomorrow." She hung up the phone and turned back to Lucas. "I completely forgot about the seniors' dance tomorrow."

"And you're covering it for the paper?"

Katie nodded.

"I'll be there as well, working on a little community project for your mother."

"For my mother?" Katie said in surprise, pleased, and he nodded mysteriously.

"She asked me to do her a favor in my capacity as police chief, and…" his voice trailed off and he shrugged. "What can I say?" He grinned and held up his hands. "I aim to please."

Katie chuckled. "I warned you my mother had your number, Lucas."

"Yeah, well I don't mind one bit. I happen to like your mother, and your aunt," he added. "Although Miss Gracie does sometimes spook me with her predictions."

Katie laughed. "You're not the only one, Lucas, and didn't we have this conversation already?" Katie frowned suddenly. "My mother wants to talk to me about something," she said, gnawing on her bottom lip and trying not to worry.

"I thought you were concerned because you thought she didn't want to talk to you and was avoiding you."

"Yeah, I was."

"So now you're worried because she *wants* to talk to you?" Lucas asked in amusement, and Katie threw the sponge at him, deliberately aiming so she'd miss. He ducked anyway.

"Like I told you before, Lucas, logic and my mother rarely go hand in hand. And sometimes I think I inherited that trait from her." Glancing around, she took a deep breath, satisfied she'd gotten the worst of the mess. "So, are you going to answer my question?" she asked, leaning against the other counter to watch him.

"Which one?"

"About whether or not you're the kind of man who doesn't believe a woman can have a career and kids?" Nervously, she crossed her arms across her chest, waiting for his answer. Lucas was never comfortable answering any of her questions, especially personal questions, but he seemed to be really contemplating his answer to this one.

She'd never had any indication that he was a man who believed one set of rules applied to men and another to women, but considering how little she knew about his past, she really couldn't be sure. And for some reason it suddenly seemed very important to her.

"No," he said quietly, then added more firmly, "not at all. Not anymore than I think a man can't have a career and kids. I think you can do anything you set out to do as long as you understand the risks and responsibilities involved. And I don't think the desire to have children or be a good parent is gender-based, nor does it preclude having a satisfying career."

He wasn't the one who didn't think a person could have a career and kids. It was his wife. And it were her concerns about *his* job that prevented them from having more children, he realized with a tinge of bitterness that he no longer could hide, even from himself.

His wife had hated his job, hated the long hours, the dedication required, hated the time he spent devoted to his cases instead of to her.

He'd desperately wanted more children and had been unbelievably close to his only son, so perhaps that's why the loss haunted him so very deeply. But his wife adamantly refused to have another child unless he gave up his job, something he'd never dream of asking her to do. Yet, she expected him to give up the career he loved in order to have another child to love. On some level that had always seemed unfair to him and had led to a lot of anger and resentment on both their parts.

Like most people who'd suffered a very personal loss, he'd tried very hard never to think of the shortcomings of his late spouse simply because it made him feel both disloyal and guilty.

But if push came to shove, and he was truly honest with himself, something he suddenly realized he hadn't been in a very long time, he understood on some level that at the heart of the matter wasn't his job, or more kids, but his wife's immaturity.

As an only child herself, his wife had been brought up to believe the world revolved around her. Used to getting everything she'd wanted from her wealthy, indulgent parents, she'd grown up never really knowing how to share or to compromise. She'd wanted and expected him to give up his own dreams to go into business with her father, knowing doing so would have probably killed him.

He was a cop, that's what he'd always been, what he'd always be, but his wife hadn't seemed to understand that. Nor, he realized now, had she cared.

Getting her own way, or pouting and punishing him until she did get her own way was her modus operandi, something that was so juvenile and immature that even now after all this time if he thought about it too long, it still riled him.

But he didn't believe in divorce—his own parents had been married over fifty years—so he realized at the time that he was the one who would have to do all the compromising, if he wanted to keep his wife happy and his marriage on track.

But he had grown weary from trying to defend both himself and his job, always wondering why his wife couldn't understand that being a cop wasn't just what he did, but an integral part of who he was.

Sort of like Katie's job, he thought, suddenly understanding in a way he hadn't before her passion for her work, because he had the same passion for *his* work. It made him look at Katie in a new light.

"Katie, can I ask you something?"

"As long as it doesn't involve spitting or burping," she said with a smile.

"You're a reporter, right?"

"Yeah," she said, wondering where he was going with this.

"It's not just what you do, but an integral part of who you are, am I right on this?"

She thought about it for a moment. "Yeah, Lucas, when you put it that way, I guess you're right." Frowning, she shook her head. "I guess I never thought of it that way." And was surprised he'd understood that about her so quickly. "But in the same way that you can't separate my aunt from her psychic abilities because that's a part of who she is as well as what she does, and the same with my mother and her astrology, I guess I'm the same way. There's nothing else I ever wanted to do except writing and reporting. I guess I always saw it as just another piece of the puzzle of what makes me...me." She shrugged. "I can't remember ever wanting anything else except to be a reporter and a mother, and hopefully successful at both."

"And you are, Katie," he assured her with a tender smile. He hesitated before asking his next question. "How do you think you'd handle it if someone, say your spouse, asked you to give it up? Your career, I mean?"

"Actually Lucas," she began slowly, "someone did basically ask me to give up my career. Or rather my dreams of a career," she corrected. "When my husband Jed and I were first married, I was so young, just out of high school, and so much in love." Laughing, she shook her head. "At that time, all that seemed important to me was getting married. Oh, I always knew I wanted to be a reporter, I think it's just in my blood, but Jed was brought up in a very traditional household. His father was old school and believed that the man was the head of the household and in charge of supporting the family."

"Which probably meant Jed didn't want you to work, right?" Lucas prodded gently, and she nodded.

"Right," she said, glancing down at the floor, before lifting her gaze to meet his. She shrugged. "Writing and reporting wasn't a career to him, it was merely a job. Not the way I thought of it at all. A job to me is something you do merely to earn money to support yourself. But a career, well a career is something you do to fill your soul. Something that's a major component of who you are. At the time it seemed so logical I guess. I loved Jed so much that giving up my own dreams hardly seemed important if it made him happy." She shrugged again and shook her head. "Now that I'm older, wiser and more mature, I realize that I probably never would have been happy in the long term if he'd forced me to give up my dreams. I mean, how could I be if I continually felt frustrated and unfulfilled? I can't help but think that by having to give up my dream it would only have lead to resentment and disappointment in the long run."

It was a hard admission, one she'd never really faced until now. It was very easy to look back at her marriage with rose-colored glasses, but age and maturity had a way of stripping away any pretense of prettiness so that she was able to see reality much clearer.

"If Jed had lived," she went on carefully, forcing herself to acknowledge something she hadn't really wanted to think about or face until now, "I think eventually it would have become a major problem between us because I personally don't think you should ever ask someone else to give up their dreams, for any reason."

"Neither do I," Lucas said softly, surprising her. She blinked up at him, wondering when he'd moved across the room. Now, he was standing right in front of her, watching her carefully. She swallowed hard before continuing.

"Mama always says any relationship is a compromise so, at the time, I thought I was just being a good, compromising wife. But then Jed was killed…" Her voice trailed off and she glanced away with a shrug. "And it was really a moot point."

"And you've felt guilty ever since, haven't you, Katie?" he asked knowingly. "For wanting something more, for knowing that as long as you were married to him you wouldn't ever be able to fulfill your other dream. But once he was gone, you knew there was nothing standing in your way. And you've carried a lot of guilt over that, haven't you?" Gently, he laid a hand on her cheek because he could see the guilt and misery on her face. He recognized it because that same guilt, that same misery, had also plagued him.

Closing her eyes, she nestled her cheek against his warm hand, marveling at how he understood things that at times she wasn't sure she understood completely.

"Yes, Lucas," she whispered quietly. "I felt enormously guilty, as if my wanting another dream had somehow caused Jed's death." Opening her eyes, she sniffled and looked at him, saw so many things in his eyes. Caring. Compassion. Understanding. They all touched her deeply, moving her in a way no man had ever moved her before.

"I don't think I've ever admitted that to anyone before," she said. "I don't think I admitted it to myself until just now." She gave an embarrassed laugh. "Actually, at the time I don't think I even thought about it, but later…later when I would go over our time together, I realized that as long as I was married to Jed, I simply had to put aside my other dreams."

"There's nothing wrong with the feelings, Katie, or with admitting them. You didn't wish or cause your husband's death—"

"No, of course not," she said with a quick shake of her head. "My logical mind understands that, but emotionally, sometimes it's harder to accept. I was in no means happy about Jed's death. I was devastated. I was a child myself, left alone to raise a child. And with no skills," she added. "So I was hardly prepared to take care of us, which is why I went back to school in the first place, and then I realized that by doing so, by making a future for Rusty and I, I was also fulfilling my lifelong dream." Her smile was sad. "One dream died, but in doing so it gave birth to another dream. And yeah, that brought on a whole lot of guilt it took me a while to come to terms with."

"Yes, but that doesn't mean you did anything to cause the first to happen."

"I realize that now, Lucas, but I think at first I wasn't quite mature enough or old enough to understand it." She hesitated. "I have to be honest with you, Lucas. I don't think I could ever again be involved with a man who didn't support my dreams, in the same way I'd support his whether I agreed with them or not. I guess I just never understood how anyone can claim to love you and then not understand or support your dreams. That doesn't make any sense to me and it's not any kind of love I understand. But I've only come to that realization in the past few years. Maturity does wonders for your common sense," she added with a wry smile. "If I love someone, I want them to be a happy, whole person and I want to help them fulfill their dreams whether they're dreams I understand or not. I don't think love gives you the right to deprive someone of their dreams."

"I agree wholeheartedly," he said, slipping his arms around her waist. He couldn't be this close to her, couldn't smell her fabulous, feminine scent or feel the comfort of her warmth without wanting to touch her, to satisfy the need and hunger that was growing day by day, hour by hour.

He smiled, drawing her closer before his mouth came down on hers, hard and hungry. She clung to his shoulders, knowing the firestorm that would start. And it did.

She could feel the hot ball of desire and yearning gather in her belly, slowly spreading through her system making her feel lethargic and warm.

Safe, she thought hazily. She felt safe, protected and cared for, things she hadn't felt in so long she'd almost forgotten what they felt like.

"Lucas," she whispered, lifting her hands to his chest. Reluctantly, she pulled away, then shook her head to clear it. "I've got popcorn to make." She sighed, torn between wanting to stay in his arms and needing to tend to her responsibility to her son and his friends. "And boys to tend to," she added a bit reluctantly.

"Yeah, I know," he added with a smile. "Okay," he said, stepping back and putting his hands on his hips. "You start the popcorn, I'll get the bowls and the butter. Just point me in the right direction." Lucas smiled, realizing he felt comfortable. Totally relaxed, and at home. Things he'd never thought he'd ever feel again, things he'd been certain were dead and buried long ago.

He'd promised himself he'd never let anyone get past his emotional guard again. He couldn't afford to. Once burned, twice shy, his dad always used to tell him.

But right now, with his heart at peace, his emotions content, and a beautiful woman puttering around the kitchen, making popcorn for the son she adored—and he had to admit, he adored as well—Lucas realized that at the moment, he couldn't think of any place he'd rather be right now, then with Katie and Rusty.

And at the moment, he was feeling much too peaceful to be frightened by it.

Chapter Eight

It wasn't until the next afternoon, several hours after Rusty's friends had gone home from the sleepover that Katie realized Rusty was acting weird. Well, weird for him, anyway.

Dressed in comfortable weekend sweats, with her hair pulled up in a ponytail, she was in the back bedroom—the one she'd turned into a makeshift home office—trying to get through the ad copy for the Halloween issue when she glanced up and saw her son standing in the doorway staring at her.

And that in itself was odd. Rusty was very rarely still. He was always in perpetual motion, so having him stand perfectly still, doing nothing and just watching her was odd.

And immediately set off motherly alarm bells.

He was supposed to be cleaning his room, Katie thought, and doing all the usual Saturday chores.

Her own legion of weekend chores—going to the market, the bank, the cleaners, the butcher's and all the other places she had to do on the weekends simply because there was no time during the week—had been put on temporary hold. She had only two weeks until the Halloween festival, and only this weekend and next to get all the edits done, so something had to be postponed and her chores were it.

So when she spotted Rusty just hanging around the doorway of her office, she immediately knew something was on his mind.

"What's up, honey?" she asked, trying to keep her voice calm and conversational as she glanced up at him.

"Uh…nothing," he said with a shrug of his shoulder, shifting from foot to foot.

"How's your room coming?" she asked and he made a face.

"I'm almost done with it," he admitted, clearly not pleased with the task.

"Did you enjoy your sleepover in the clubhouse?"

Pleasure swept over his face and he grinned. "Yeah, it was so awesome. Can I have another sleepover? Soon?"

Katie chuckled. "Aren't you staying at Sean's tonight?"

"Yeah, so I guess that's a sleepover, huh?"

"Have you got something else on your mind, honey?"

"Nah…." He shifted, glanced down at his battered

tennis shoes, then up at her. "Well, maybe." He hesitated a moment. "Can I…uh…ask you a question, Ma?"

"You can ask me anything, honey, you know that." She smiled at him. "I can't guarantee I'll always know the answer, but I'll always tell you the truth."

Shifting his weight again, he glanced down at his shoes then shoved his hands in the pockets of his ragged jeans. "Do you…uh…think…I mean…you…uh…think…Lucas is nice, isn't he?" he asked, daring a glance at her from under his lashes.

Warning bells began to hum inside her head but she tried not to show them, wondering where this question was coming from, and more importantly, why Rusty was asking it.

"Yes, honey," she said carefully. "Lucas is a very nice man. I think you're very lucky to have him for a buddy, don't you?" she asked, watching her son's face carefully.

His grin flashed as he slouched against the doorjamb. "Yeah, real lucky," he said with a laugh that brightened his green eyes. "All the guys are kinda like jealous, I think just because Lucas is so awesome." His grin widened. "And he's *my* buddy," he said proudly, staking proprietary ownership over Lucas.

"So you think Lucas is awesome," Katie repeated in relief, nodding at Rusty.

"Yeah. He's just so cool," Rusty went on quickly, excitement animating his words. "He knows about all kinds of stuff, Ma. He knows about fishing, and about building stuff like the clubhouse. And he never, like, yells or loses his patience or gets mad when I do something wrong like Sean's dad."

"Sean's dad yells?" Katie asked in surprise and Rusty snorted.

"He's a champion yeller, Ma," he admitted with a crooked grin. "But he doesn't mean it. Sometimes we think he does it just to be funny." His shoulders moved restlessly again. "Sean's ma says he just like hearing his own voice."

Katie smothered a smile. "Yeah, well, maybe you'd better keep that tidbit of information to yourself, honey." Relieved, she rested her chin on her hand. "So does this mean you like having Lucas as your buddy?"

"Yeah, sure," Rusty said with another shrug, trying to appear nonchalant, but she was heartily afraid her son had a very bad case of hero worship. Katie sighed. She knew the feeling.

"So then you want Lucas to keep being your buddy? Or would you rather have someone else, honey?"

"No! I don't want any other buddy, Ma, I only want Lucas for my buddy."

"Okay, okay," she said carefully, wondering where all this emotion was coming from. "I was just wondering, honey. I wasn't certain how well you and Lucas had been getting along. I know it seems like you get along great…" Her voice trailed off and she shrugged. "But sometimes looks can be deceiving."

"We do get along great, Ma. Honest," Rusty insisted. "And I don't want no one else for my buddy. Ever," Rusty said, crossing his arms across his chest defiantly.

"So you like Lucas, then?" Katie asked carefully.

"Yeah, a lot." He hesitated, scuffing the toe of his tennis shoe on the floor for a moment before looking up at her, his eyes swimming with some emotion she wasn't sure she recognized. "Do you…uh…like him, Ma?" His gaze met hers and she realized for some reason this seemed important to him as well.

"Well, Rusty, I don't think it really matters if I like Lucas or not. He's your buddy, remember?"

"Yeah, but…I mean you don't…like…dislike him or anything do you?" he asked with a confused frown.

She laughed, unwilling to admit to her son her feelings for Lucas were at the opposite spectrum of dislike. She was still trying to figure them out for herself. "Yes, honey, I like Lucas," she admitted. "I think he's been a very good buddy to you, and he's also become a friend to me."

"A friend," Rusty repeated, trying to keep the disgust out of his voice. Even he knew that if a girl wanted to be your friend it wasn't good. Sean had said that was like the kiss of death or something. Cow cakes!

"Are you sure nothing is wrong, honey?"

"Nah, it's just…could I ask you another question?"

"Sure, honey." Apparently he was taking lessons from her mother and aunt, and was going to get to this in his own good time.

"Well…uh…" His face flushed pink and he went back to staring at his shoes. "The other night…I…uh… kinda…saw…you…uh…kiss Lucas. I wasn't spying or nuthin'," he added quickly. "But I…uh…was just… wondering…" His voice trailed off and he shrugged, clearly embarrassed and uncomfortable and not wanting to look at her.

"Oh honey, I'm sorry." Her heart was knocking again, like a piston this time as the sticky fingers of guilt squeezed at her heart. So that's what all this was about. She should have known, and been more sensitive.

It had been just her and him for so long that the idea of seeing her with another man—kissing a man—had probably brought up a whole host of emotions Rusty had no idea how to cope with. Maybe he'd been jealous, or confused, or worse, scared. The guilt squeezed harder and Katie cursed herself for not being more sensitive and aware of her son's feelings.

"Did it upset you to see me kissing Lucas?" she asked softly.

"Nah…it didn't like…upset me…or nothing," he admitted, then shrugged again. "Sean's mom and dad are always kissing," he revealed with another snort. "It's like really disgusting and gross." He made an appropriate face to indicate his displeasure. "But I was just wondering…like, how come you…uh…kissed Lucas?" He lifted his chin and looked at her.

"Well, honey, remember I told you Lucas was my friend," she began slowly, and he nodded. "Well, honey, sometimes friends kiss."

"Yuck," he said, swiping a hand across his mouth in horror.

She laughed. "Yeah, I know honey, but I promise you when you get a little bit older you're going to meet a girl and you and her are going to become friends, and maybe one day you're going to want to kiss her."

"Kiss a girl?" he repeated, his eyes going wide in utter horror. "I'd rather kiss a rabid rat," he said, clutching his stomach and making gagging sounds. Katie laughed.

"I promise one day you'll change your mind," she assured him and he shook his head furiously.

"Uh-uh, I'm never kissing a girl and I don't want any girls for friends, either." He paused for a moment and she knew he was thinking. "So, Ma, kissing Lucas was kind of just like when you used to kiss Mr. Riley?"

"Mr. Riley?" Katie repeated, confused, then it dawned on her. "Oh, you mean the maintenance man who always came to fix stuff when we lived in Madison?"

"Yeah, that Mr. Riley."

Katie smiled. Mr. Riley was sixty if he was a day, and a sweetheart. He was the maintenance man at the university, but did side jobs to supplement his Social Security income. Except no matter what he fixed for her, he refused to take any money. Katie had adored him and kissed him on the cheek every time he fixed something for her.

"Yeah, honey, I guess you could say it was kind of like when I kissed Mr. Riley. He was my friend, too." It wasn't quite the same thing, she realized, but if this answer would ease Rusty's concerns, it would have to do for the moment.

How could she explain her relationship with Lucas and her feelings when she wasn't certain she understood it herself?

"Yeah, okay," Rusty said, suddenly looking dejected. "I'm gonna go finish my room," he said, turning from the doorway and leaving Katie feeling as if she'd somehow gotten all the answers on a big test wrong.

"Rusty?"

He turned back. "Yeah?"

"Is there anything else that's bothering you?"

He thought about it for a minute. "Do I got a tie?"

"A tie?" Katie repeated, blinking at him in confusion. "You mean a tie like you wear when you wear a white shirt?"

"Yeah."

"Sure you do, honey. It's in the bottom drawer in your dresser, right hand side. Why?"

He shrugged. "Sean's ma said she'd take us to the pancake breakfast tomorrow morning, but she says we gotta wear stupid, dorky ties to church."

"Sounds like a good idea to me," she said, earning a face from her son. "Okay, you go finish your room while I try to finish these edits." She glanced at her watch. "I have to be at the seniors' dance around five thirty, so I'll drop you off at Sean's on the way, okay?"

He shrugged. "Yeah, sure."

"And Rusty?"

"Yeah?"

"I love you, honey."

"Love you, too," he mumbled as he bolted toward his room, leaving Katie staring after him.

Boys and men should come with a handbook, Katie thought with a weary sigh. It would certainly make a woman's life simpler.

* * *

"Did you ask her?" Sean demanded of Rusty later that afternoon. "Huh? Did you?" Huddled together on the floor of Sean's bedroom, they'd shut the door to make certain they had privacy so they could discuss their latest project.

"I asked her," Rusty admitted dejectedly, slumping back against Sean's unmade bed. There were two twin beds in the room, both unmade, separated by a small nightstand with a lamp. The twin beds came in handy for sleepovers and for piling things on when Sean didn't feel like cleaning his room—which was often.

"So what did she say?"

"She said Lucas is just…a friend," Rusty admitted, trying not to scowl.

"A friend? She said that?" he asked in disbelief. "That Lucas was just…a *friend?*"

Rusty nodded dismally.

"Bummer," Sean slumped back against the spare bed before turning to his friend. "Did you ask her about kissing him?"

Rusty nodded, then shrugged. "Yeah. My ma said that sometimes friends…kiss friends."

Sean's eyes went wide in disbelief. "Get outta here, really?"

Rusty nodded dismally. "Really."

"Well, I ain't never kissing any of my friends," Sean said, making a face as he shook his head feverishly. "That's just gross."

Rusty sighed. "I know."

"So what are we going to do?"

Rusty shook his head, then shrugged. "Dunno."

Crossing his arms across his chest, Sean stared hard at his friend. "Well, we gotta do something if you want Lucas to be your dad, because it doesn't look so good right now. If your ma likes him just as a friend, maybe she just…you know…needs to spend more time with him or something."

"Yeah, maybe," Rusty said with a scowl.

"Hey, I got an idea," Sean said, brightening. "A really good idea, and it'll probably even work." He frowned. "Maybe."

"Really?" Rusty said hopefully.

"Yeah." Sean grinned, revealing several missing front teeth. "Really." He motioned Rusty closer so they wouldn't be overheard, then bent to whisper in Rusty's ear. "Here's what we gotta do."

Cooper's Cove had an active and vital seniors' club that participated in a great many of the town's activities while hosting quite a few of their own.

In spite of their numerous activities, most of which were primarily fund-raisers for a seniors' center, the seniors held most of their functions in the gymnasium of the grammar school or the basement of the church until enough funds could be raised or secured to build their own center.

After dropping Rusty off at Sean's, Katie headed over to the dance. By the time she found a parking space, grabbed her notepad and headed into the school, the dance was already underway.

At the door right outside the gymnasium, Francis Cushing, the longtime treasurer of the seniors' club, sat taking tickets. A retired concert violinist with six grown children, at eighty-five Francis was still active, and still played in a quartet of musicians every week. For as long as Katie could remember, Francis had been giving free music lessons to any child who wanted them.

Unfortunately, Katie's own musical aspirations had lasted less than a week before Francis kindly and gently told her mother that Katie couldn't carry a tune even if she had an empty suitcase.

So much for her budding musical career, Katie mused, but she'd been secretly thrilled because it freed her up after school so she could spend more time at the newspaper office—her real love.

"Evening, Katherine," Francis said with a smile. "Now you know you don't have to pay admission, not while you're working the dance for the newspaper."

"I know," Katie admitted with a laugh, handing the bill to Francis anyway. "But I still want to make a contribution."

"Why, Katherine, thank you. The seniors truly appreciate your donation." Francis tucked the bill into her metal cash box, then leaned across it and lowered her voice. "And you tell your mama I'm rooting for her."

"Rooting for her?" Katie repeated with a frown.

"Why, yes, dear. In her run for mayor."

Katie managed to suppress a groan—but just barely. "Uh…Francis, who told you Mama was running for mayor?"

"Why your mother did. Just a few moments ago." Francis glanced around to make certain no one could hear her. "Said she's going to announce her candidacy at the Halloween Festival, but she wanted a few of her close friends to know in advance."

Close friends? Good Lord, everyone in town was a close friend of her mother's, Katie thought with a scowl, which meant Louella had probably already told everyone in town.

Except her.

Still smiling, Francis patted her braids. "I don't know how Mayor Hannity is going to take the news. But new blood is always a good thing, don't you think, Katherine?"

Katie nodded, not trusting herself to speak, fearing a rash of words that might make Francis blush would start spilling from her mouth.

"Now you go on in and have a good time, Katherine," Francis instructed. "We've got a nice band tonight, and I'm sure you'll enjoy yourself. Oh, and Katherine, be careful where you step," Francis warned with a slight frown. "Patience insisted on bringing Leonardo with her tonight."

"Leonardo?" Katie tried not to laugh. This was a bit of gossip she hadn't heard. Patience apparently had a new man in her life.

Francis heaved a weary sigh. "Her new dog. Drags that poor little thing with her everywhere," Francis said with a cluck of her tongue. "Tonight she's got him trussed up in a bow tie and a tuxedo jacket."

"Well, it is a Halloween dance," Katie pointed out, trying not to laugh.

"I suppose so," Francis conceded, always wanting to be fair. "Now you go on in and have yourself a good time."

"Thanks," Katie said, yanking open one of the double doors to slip inside the gymnasium where it was still apparently 1941, judging from the big band sound that was wafting through the air.

The senior decorating committee had done a fine job making the gym look like a haunted house. The band was stationed on the pullout stage, several inches off the ground and at the far end of the gym. Colored spotlights of black and orange floated and crisscrossed over the band members, illuminating them in Halloween hues.

Ghosts, goblins and an assortment of other spooky creatures were grinning from the walls. A white spider web stretched high across the entire ceiling—caught in it were several black plastic spiders the size of Montana.

Along the far side of the gym a table was set up with cold refreshments and hot coffee. Along a side wall, another table was set up as a dessert buffet.

The gymnasium was packed, as usual, since most of the town showed up for the monthly seniors' dance, not just the seniors. As usual, the females outnumbered the males by probably three to one, but a smattering of couples moved on the dance floor, while a shiny disco mirrored ball spun overhead, giving the appearance of a old-fashioned ballroom.

Katie quickly scanned the crowd, waved to Patience, who was on the dance floor doing a two-step with Leonardo, before waving and blowing a kiss to the mayor, who was engaged in a heated debate with the fire chief over at the dessert table, but it was her mother she was looking for. She finally spotted her mother and her aunt near the refreshment table.

Determined to talk to her mother and get to the bottom of this "running for mayor" business, Katie headed over.

"Mama," Katie said, kissing her cheek.

"Katherine, dear, I'm so glad you made it." Her mom beamed at her. "It's a lovely evening, isn't it, dear?"

"Yes, Mama, it is." Katie leaned over and kissed her aunt. "Aunt Gracie."

"Sweetheart, it's good to see you." Gracie looked beyond Katie. "Where's Rusty tonight?"

"I dropped him off at Sean's. They're having a sleepover tonight and then Sean's mother's taking them to the pancake breakfast at church in the morning."

"We're going to the pancake breakfast in the morning, too," Louella said with a smile, patting her perfectly coiffed hair. "So I'll get to see my favorite grandson."

"He's your only grandson," Gracie pointed out with a chuckle, waving to the librarian across the gym.

"Uh…Mama, could I talk to you for a minute?"

"Why of course." Her mother looked puzzled. "Is something wrong, dear? You're looking a little peaked." Louella patted Katie's cheek. "But that's to be expected, dear, considering," her mother added mysteriously. "But I don't want you to worry. Everything is going to be fine. Eventually."

Katie took a deep breath, counted to ten—twice—before speaking. "Mama, what are you talking about?"

Louella sighed. "Well, dear, remember last night on the phone I told you that I wanted to talk to you?"

"Yes," Katie said carefully, surprised that her mother remembered their conversation last night.

"Well, dear, I read your astrological chart for the upcoming month, and I'm afraid you're going to have some very trying times in the next few weeks."

"Really?" Katie said, not in the least bit surprised, considering at the moment it was her mother who was giving her one of those trying times.

"Yes, dear." Her mother's brows drew together. "I'm afraid one of the men in your life is going to be quite upset with you. There's going to be a terrible row, I'm afraid."

"One of the men in my life?" Katie said with a lift of her brow and a chuckle. "Mama, you make it sound like I've got legions of men in my life."

"Well, dear, when you think about it, you do. Your uncle, Rusty, Lucas, the mayor, Mr. Hensen—"

Katie held up her hand before her mother named every male in town. "Okay, so one of the men in my life is going to be upset with me. And there's going to be a terrible row with him. Do you want to tell me who or why?"

"I'm afraid the 'who,' dear, is a bit fuzzy, but the 'why' is a bit clearer. It's going to be some kind of misunderstanding I believe, causing a rift and a breach of trust." At the alarmed look on Katie's face, Louella sought to soothe, patting her cheek again. "But don't worry, dear, honestly. It will all work out. Eventually," her mother added with another delicate little frown.

Small crystals of ice had begun forming in Katie's belly and she wondered if what happened with Rusty this afternoon, their discussion about her kissing Lucas, was what her mother had seen in her astrological chart.

The thought brought on a shiver and she realized she

was overreacting. Wouldn't she have known if he was truly upset about something? Not convinced, Katie realized there was nothing she could do about it at the moment, so for now, she'd better concentrate on her other immediate problem—her mother.

"Oh, and Katie dear, I'll need you to reserve at least two pages of ad space for me in the Halloween issue."

"Why?" Katie asked suspiciously and her mother smiled serenely.

"Well, dear, if I'm going to run for mayor I think an official announcement is in order, don't you?"

Katie quickly counted to ten before speaking. "Mama, when did you decide to run for mayor. And more importantly, *why?*"

"When?" her mother repeated, bewildered. "Well, Katie dear I told you all about this. Last week. Don't you remember, dear?" Her mother's eyes clouded. "Didn't I?" she asked weakly and Katie shook her head.

"No, Mama," she said gently, touching her mother's arm in concern. "You didn't tell me about it. Patience told me. Francis told me, but you never told me. And I think this is too serious for us not to at least discuss. Taking on the town is a lot more difficult and demanding than running the Astrology Parlor. It's something I think you need to seriously think about before making a firm decision."

"Well, yes, of course, dear. But I could have sworn I told you…" Louella's voice trailed off and her gaze went over Katie's shoulder. "Well, for goodness sake, look at that. It's Lucas and Rusty and Sean and, why it looks like the whole basketball team."

"Rusty?" Katie repeated, turning around. Her jaw

dropped open and she merely stared as Lucas led the boys, all of whom looked like someone had spit shined and polished them to within an inch of their lives, into the gym. Their hair was combed, and they were all dressed in white shirts and ties.

"What do you think they're doing here, dear?"

Katie sighed. "I don't know, Mama, but let's go find out."

With her mother and her aunt trailing in her wake, Katie made her way through the crowd of dancers to the other side of the gym where Lucas and the boys were standing like soldiers on sentry.

"Lucas," she said, glancing at her son who was grinning from ear to ear. "I suppose there is a very good reason why you and the boys are here?"

He smiled at her, then leaned forward to kiss her mother and her aunt hello before bringing his gaze back to hers.

"There is, Katie. Do you remember the morning I dropped off Rusty's time capsule? When your mother asked me if I could…uh…use my position as police chief to sort of find some more male escorts for the seniors' dance since the women always outnumbered the men?"

"Yeah," Katie said carefully. "I remember."

"Well, I'd like you to meet the new escorts." He turned toward the boys who were all desperately trying not to fidget.

"It's a community service project, Ma," Rusty said with a careless shrug. "For the town," he added. "And don't worry, we all learned how to dance."

"Dance?" Katie repeated, a bit shocked. "You learned how to dance?"

"Yeah," Rusty said, craning his neck and fiddling with his tie. "Lucas taught us." He shrugged. "He said all men need to know how to dance. And besides, everyone who is part of the town should volunteer to do what they can to help others, using whatever special skills they got. Lucas says everyone has special skills and they should use them to help others. You know, like Mrs. Cushing gives free music lessons and stuff." Rusty cast another admiring glance at Lucas, as he recited almost verbatim what Lucas had told him. "It's called being a good citizen."

"A good citizen?" Katie repeated, pride swamping her. "I'm very proud of you, sweetheart," she said, forgetting that all his friends were standing right there watching as she leaned over to kiss him.

"Ma!" Rearing back, Rusty raised his hands to block her. "You can't kiss me," he hissed in horror, turning beet red and glancing back at the guys. "No kissing me in public, remember?"

"Oh, yeah, I'm sorry," she said, trying not to grin. "I forgot. But I'm still very proud of you."

"Yeah, thanks, Ma," Rusty mumbled, terrified she was going to try to kiss him again. Awkwardly, he stepped toward Louella and held out his arms. "Uh…Grandma, do you wanna…like…uh…dance or something?"

"Oh, dear, yes, I'd love to dance." Louella's eyes swam and she clapped her hands in delight. "This is just wonderful. Absolutely wonderful, Lucas." She leaned up on tiptoe to kiss Lucas's cheek. "I must confess I do believe I'm in falling love with you," Louella teased and Katie merely sighed. She knew the feeling.

* * *

"You look beat," Lucas whispered in Katie's ear as they slowly made their way around the dance floor as the dance finally wound down. They were moving to the strains of an old forties ballad that had made Katie feel both warm and nostalgic.

"I am," she admitted, lazily glancing up at him with a smile. His arms were comfortable around her, lulling her into a lethargic state. "After you left last night I couldn't really sleep knowing the boys were outside in the clubhouse." She shrugged at his lifted brow. "Yeah, I know they were safe and sound asleep, but I was just worried about them being outside all night."

"Mother's prerogative," he said simply, smiling down at her as he pulled her a bit closer until her body was pressed the length of his. He could feel his blood begin to stir and his mind to cloud just having her near. Holding her so close, he could smell her, that lingering sultry scent that had been driving him mad since the moment he met her.

"After the boys finally left this morning, I cleaned the house a bit, then worked on the Halloween edits." She stifled a yawn. "I worked until it was time to come to the dance."

"And are you working after the dance?" Lucas asked glancing down at her. Her mouth was only inches from his, and if he leaned forward just a bit, he could brush his mouth against hers. Fearing he might do just that Lucas struggled to keep his mind on their conversation and his feelings in check.

Katie shook her head. "I thought I might, but to tell

you the truth, I'm too tired. I actually think I'm going to take the night off, or rather what's left of it," she added with a laugh, realizing it was almost ten o'clock. "Rusty's staying overnight at Sean's, so I thought I'd just get one good full night's sleep and start back in on the edits in the morning. After I deal with my mother."

"Your mother? What's wrong with your mother?" he asked drawing back to look at her as the song ended. Keeping his hand around her waist, he guided her to the side of the dance floor and out of the way of the other dancers.

"She's decided to run for mayor," she said, trying not to scowl.

"Mayor?" Lucas shook his head, confused. "But Katie, I thought you said since your mom's stroke she's had trouble with her short term memory. Can she really handle running the town?"

"No," Katie said with a laugh. "But I guess someone forgot to tell Mama that. I don't think she really wants to *be* mayor, I think this has something to do with Mayor Hannity. Something personal. He and Mama have been 'keeping company,' as she says, for almost twenty years now, and apparently they recently had some kind of falling out, and the next thing I know, Mama's decided to run for his job."

"Ahh, so that's how it is." He kept his hand at her waist, unwilling to let her go, aware that they were standing in full view of most of the town. "Want me to nose around the mayor and see what I can find out?" he asked, as the band announced the last song of the evening.

"You'd do that?" she asked, glancing up at him in

surprise. He was so close, and she was so tired, it was almost too tempting to have his warm, solid presence so close. The urge to just lean against him, to let go of every worry in her mind and just let her guard down and relax against Lucas was nearly overwhelming.

"Of course," Lucas said with a smile. "Why not?"

She shrugged, feeling off balance because he was so close and her resistance was so depleted. "I don't know, I thought maybe male loyalty or something might prevent it."

"Nope," Lucas said. "I seemed to have missed the male loyalty gene. Besides, I happen to adore your mother," he said, brushing a strand of hair off her face and letting his finger linger on her cheek. "And I agree with you that running for mayor might not be the best thing for her. Besides, I happen to think the mayor's doing a fine job."

"I agree with you on both counts," Katie said slowly. With the warmth of his touch lingering on her cheek, she just wanted to nestle her cheek against his hand, close her eyes and do nothing but feel.

"Listen, Katie…" Lucas hesitated. "I know you're beat, but I was going to ask you if you wanted to go out for a drink or some coffee or maybe something to eat, but if you're too tired—"

"No, actually, I think I'd like that," she admitted, meeting his gaze and seeing so many things that stirred and touched her heart. Her heart began a two-step when she realized what he was asking—he was asking to see *her,* not Rusty. Her. Alone.

The mere thought had her stomach doing a jig. In all

this time, they'd never been alone and Lucas had never made any attempt to see her without Rusty being present since he was after all, Rusty's buddy. But she knew now that they'd crossed some kind of bridge, some kind of barrier and were about to embark on something that might change her—and their relationship—forever.

"Everything in town is closed by now, Lucas," she said carefully, "so why don't you just come by the house and I can make some us some coffee and something to eat."

"I'd like that," he said softly, aching to touch her but aware they were in full view of the whole town. Trying to keep his mind on the task at hand, Lucas's gaze searched the gym. "But I've got to round up all the boys and drive them home first."

"And I've got to drive Mama and Aunt Gracie home."

"So how about if I meet you at your house in say… half an hour?"

"That will be great," she assured him. "I'll be waiting."

Chapter Nine

By the time Katie got home, she was a bundle of nerves. It had been so long since she'd been alone with a man, so long since she'd felt any of the feelings Lucas stirred in her, she wasn't quite certain what to do with herself.

To keep her mind off her jangled nerves, Katie concentrated on the practical. The moment she got home, she started a fresh pot of coffee, checked the kitchen to make sure it wasn't a total disaster area, then went into the family room to start a fire in the fireplace. It was nippy enough now that a roaring fire would not only take the chill out of the air, but also would make things seem a bit cozier.

She dashed into her bedroom to check her appearance and to change. She'd worn a dress to the dance, but now slipped into a comfortable pair of jeans and an oversize sweater. She pulled the pins out of her hair and brushed it through, letting it fall free. She thought about redoing what little bit of makeup she had on, then decided against it, settling for another spritz of her favorite perfume.

She'd just taken a deep breath and checked herself out in the full-length mirror when the doorbell rang.

Pressing a hand to her stomach to try to steady it, she took a deep breath, then hurried to the door, pulling it open.

"Just in time, I think the coffee's just about done," she said with a shaky smile, letting Lucas in and cursing the nerves that were dancing over her skin, almost making her shiver.

"Smells great," he said as he followed her back to the kitchen, loosening his tie and collar along the way.

"Have a seat in the family room," she said, gesturing him toward the couch. "I lit a fire. It's the first one of the season."

"It's terrific," he said, taking off his suit jacket and laying it on the back of the couch. His tie followed, and he unbuttoned his shirt collar, opening it to let his neck breathe.

He stood in front of the fireplace for a moment, watching the flames, aware of how quiet it was in the house, and how alone they were.

As she got out coffee mugs, cream and sugar and placed everything on a tray, Lucas came to help her, taking the tray from her hands. Their fingers brushed and it was as if a jolt of electricity shot through both of them. Katie's gaze flew to his and held. She was surprised by the warmth and softness in his eyes. Gone was the pain and anguish she so frequently saw, and she couldn't help it, she relaxed a bit, knowing he seemed relaxed.

She followed him to the couch, sitting down next to him as he handed her a mug of coffee and took one for himself.

"It's so quiet in the house it's almost spooky," she said with a laugh as she sipped her coffee. "It's rare when Rusty isn't here, blaring the television, or his video games or the radio." Aware of how close Lucas was to her, Katie stared into her coffee mug. "Lucas, I don't know how to thank you for everything you've done for Rusty." She dared to look at him, and found him watching her curiously. He set his mug down, and sat back, laying his arm around the back of the couch. "I don't know that I ever realized how much Rusty needed an adult male's influence. At least not until he met you." She took a sip of her coffee because her throat was suddenly dry, then set her mug on the table in front of her.

"Well, like I said, Katie," Lucas began softly, playing with the silky tips of the back of her hair. It was just as soft as he'd always imagined. "He's a terrific kid and you've done a terrific job with him."

"Thanks." Her heart was banging against her ribs so fast and hard she feared he might hear it. Not one to play coy, Katie decided she'd had enough of being nervous. "Lucas, look, I'm sorry, I'm not very good at this."

He smiled at her. "Good at what?"

She sighed. "Good at making small talk with a man." She shrugged. "I don't exactly have a wealth of experience when it comes to men, and I'm afraid even if I did, it's been so long since I've been alone with a man I'm just woefully out of practice."

"You're nervous," he said gently, pleased and touched when she nodded.

"I am," she admitted, glancing up at him.

Touched and humbled beyond measure that she could be so nervous, and look so vulnerable because of him, he took her hands in his. "Relax, Katie," he said softly, lifting her hands to kiss her fingertips. "There's nothing to be nervous about," he said softly, releasing her hands to caress her cheek, feeling his own heart jump when she nestled her face against his hand in welcome.

"Did I ever tell you how much I love your perfume?" he asked, letting his hand slide from her cheek to caress her neck. Her skin was like silk and warmed under his touch. "That first night we met, when I caught you digging up my yard, I swore I smelled your scent all night long. It kept me awake," he admitted with a smile. "You're trembling," he said quietly and her eyes opened and she smiled wryly.

"Yeah, I am." She shrugged, trying to dismiss her nerves. "My perfume might make you crazy, but when you touch me it makes me crazy," she admitted without a hint of embarrassment.

"And that scares you?"

"Lots of things scare me, Lucas, but you're not one of them." She lifted her chin, forced herself to meet and hold his gaze. She could feel her pulse speed up, could feel the hot seed of need and desire begin to plant itself deep inside.

"I'm glad." He couldn't resist any longer. She was

so close and the tight rein of control he'd had on himself for so long suddenly seemed to be slipping and he knew there was nothing he could do about it.

He bent his head to gently nibble at the corner of her mouth and heard her soft sigh of acquiescence. It only fueled and flamed the need and desire coursing through him.

"Lucas," she murmured, reaching for him, sliding her hand around his neck and pulling his mouth down fully on hers. "You're driving me crazy."

Her words set off a flash fire inside of him that threatened to burn him up from the inside out. Fighting for breath, for sanity, he dragged her closer, crushing her mouth under his.

His blood went straight to boil, overloading his system as he dragged her yet closer, wanting to mate, to meld with her, to become one. It had been a desperate need growing from the moment he'd laid eyes on her, and now, the desire had been unleashed and he knew he was hopeless to stop it.

"Katie." Gently, his hands bracketed her face as his gaze held hers. "Beautiful, you're so beautiful." Awed and humbled by the emotions shimmering in her eyes, the trust and vulnerability, he slid his fingers through the sensuous silk of her hair, the silk he'd dreamed of, fantasized about night after night until he thought he'd go mad.

He murmured her name like a prayer, a plea. Anchoring his fingers in the silk of her hair, he tilted her head back to tease and caress her mouth with his, taking the kiss deeper, then deeper still until the blood was pounding in his ears, his limbs, his loins.

"Lucas," she murmured his name, fisting her own hands in his hair, dragging him closer, fearing she'd slide off the edge of the world if she didn't. They slid down on the couch together, his body half covering hers.

Her heart was slamming inside her breast as desire, dark and dangerous, slid through her like a magic potion, awakening all the needs and desires, all the things she'd kept buried for so long.

She wanted this now, wanted to feel this joy, this pleasure, this man in her arms, in her body.

When his mouth slid from her lips to her neck, caressing, nibbling, arousing, she could only moan softly, holding him tightly, silently pleading for more.

She shuddered, then sighed when his warm hand slid under her sweater and skin met skin. The shudder went straight through to her heart, and his heart gave a shuddering sigh in return.

She reached down, pulled the hem of her sweater up and over her head, tossed it across the floor, her gaze never leaving his. She would remember the look in his eyes forever. Desire, fresh and hot, flared and darkened his gaze until she was certain she might ignite from all the heat.

"Katie," he said her name reverently, a soft prayer in the quiet room. The logs in the fireplace shifted, sent a spray of sparks flying upward even as he caressed her, from shoulder to waist, bare hand to bare skin until she was moaning softly, wanting, begging for more, arching upward toward him, pressing her body against his, wanting to ease the ache that had only grown with each moment of his touch.

When his mouth, soft and sweet, dipped into the gentle hollow between her breasts, she moaned softly, slipping the straps of her bra off her shoulders to give him better access.

Her eyes closed and she gasped as his mouth closed over her breast, warm and wet, urging her up and up until she was certain she would go mad.

Need spiraled through her, and she clutched at the back of his shirt, dragging it up so she, too, could feel flesh against flesh. Her hands smoothed under his shirt, caressed the skin until she had him nearly mad. Her hands slid up and down his back, wanting more, needing to feel his arousal even as she felt her own.

"Lucas, I want you." Her voice was a husky moan as he slid his hand from her shoulder to her waist in a teasing, caressing motion. Unbearable heat and love poured through her and she clung tighter to him when he drew back to look into her eyes as he unsnapped her jeans.

The moan ripped from her when his mouth touched the bare, tender skin exposed by her zipper. He drew her jeans off, kissing every bare, exposed inch as he did, before tossing her jeans in the heap of clothes on the floor.

For a moment, he merely looked at her, then ran a finger, just one gentle finger, over her lips, down her chin, her shoulder, across the curve of her breast, down the flat of her bare belly, then down one leg, and up the other, first the inside, then the outside.

She was warm, wet and welcoming, and the knowledge almost pushed him past reason as his fingers expertly caressed her, sliding inside her welcoming body until her eyes glazed with numbing desire. He drove her higher, then higher still, until a moan ripped through her as she hit the peak and spilled over him.

She was nearly panting when she reached up to hook her arm around his neck and drag him back down to her, fusing her mouth with his for one hot moment.

"Off," she murmured, tugging his shirt with a free hand, and he obliged, slipping out of his shirt, and then his pants, so that he could cover her naked body with his own.

He had to stop, to take a deep breath, to fill his aching lungs with air or else he'd go mad from the feel of that soft, feminine body, smooth as silk, slid against him.

Gently, he pushed her hair off her face, then stroked the length, wanting to prolong this pleasure, this madness. God, how he loved the feel of her hair. He'd never grow tired of the feel of it sliding through his fingers, rubbing against his skin.

She arched upward, kissing every inch her mouth could reach, wanting to taste him, to feel him, to be filled by him. To mate with the man she loved, to know the ultimate beauty of that love.

"Lucas." She only said his name, but it was enough. He lifted her gently, and she arched in welcome, causing him to mutter a curse as her legs wrapped around him like a vise.

He buried his face in the silky skin of her neck even as he slowly buried himself inside of her, certain he would lose his mind from pleasure, the welcoming of her. He felt entirely possessive and protective of this woman who'd somehow managed to fill his heart and his mind, and stir his senses. The feelings threatened to overwhelm him, blinding him, deafening him to everything but the feel and touch of her.

"Lucas." The word gasped out as she began to move beneath him, pure joy sliding through her as the rhythm of love nearly took her to the edge.

She clung to him, pressing her lips to him anywhere, everywhere, wanting this total connection, this total mating as the rhythm increased and they rocked against one another, faster and faster.

"Lucas, Lucas." Her eyes closed, and she felt salty tears behind her lids for this beauty he'd given to her, for the joy of knowing and feeling love again.

She clung tighter to him, digging her fingers into his bare back, urging him on, whispering his name like a prayer over and over until he was nearly blind, dazed and delirious.

"Katie." Her name wrenched from him as she went taut, then shuddered around him, dragging him over the edge of reason with her.

A log shifted, broke in half, then clattered to the bottom of the fireplace. The sound stirred her and Katie opened her eyes. She had no idea how long she'd been dozing, but it had grown chilly in the room, and the fire was half the size it originally was.

But she felt warm and cozy nestled naked in the crook of Lucas's arm. She turned her head to look at him, to admire his profile, his strong, handsome features, her heart nearly overflowing with love. Unable to resist, she ran a hand over his bare chest, feeling the steady, soothing beat of his heart.

"I think our coffee's probably gone cold," she said, planting a kiss on his shoulder. "Would you like me to make some more?"

"No, thanks." His voice was clipped, curt, and he didn't look at her, he just kept staring up at the ceiling.

She touched his shoulder even as her own heart began to hammer in fear. "Lucas, what's wrong?"

He sat up abruptly, dragging his hands through his hair. "Katie, look, I'm sorry."

"Sorry?" she repeated, confused. The first pebble of pain slid under her heart, making it ache. But pride refused to allow her to show it. "Sorry for what, Lucas?" she asked softly.

"For this…" He waved his arm in the air. "For everything."

"You mean for making love with me?" she asked quietly, sitting up and dragging the afghan from the back of the couch to wrap around her. She was suddenly very cold.

"This shouldn't have happened," he snapped, reaching for his shirt off the pile and yanking it free. He was furious with himself. "I shouldn't have let this happen."

"It seems to me you weren't the only one involved, Lucas. I let it happen, too."

"Yeah, then we both should have known better," he snapped, shoving his arms into his shirt and buttoning it. He was disgusted with himself, disgusted that he'd let his emotions overrule his common sense. He knew better, didn't he? Knew that no good could come of this?

"Well, I'm sorry to disappoint you, Lucas, but I'm not sorry this happened," she said, blinking back the hot flash of tears that burned her eyes. "And I'm sorry that you are."

"Katie, look—" he broke off when he looked at her, saw her stricken face, and cursed himself six ways to Sunday. He'd hurt her, damn it, hurt her and he'd never intended to. He'd been trying to protect her, to protect her and Rusty by keeping his emotional distance, but something had happened with her, something that had never happened with another woman. His emotions overruled and overpowered his common sense. And because of it, he'd ended up doing the one thing he never wanted to do—hurt Katie.

"Listen." He dragged his hands through his hair and took a deep breath, not certain what to say or how to say it. But he was dangerously close to losing what little shred of control he had, and he couldn't risk it, couldn't tell her what was in his heart. It was too painful, for him, for her. It was better this way, better to keep his distance, to forget her, forget this ever happened.

But it had happened, giving him a glimpse of what life could be like if he ever allowed himself to feel again.

No! His mind snapped, and his heart began to ache, fresh and raw, in a way it hadn't ached since those first early days when he'd been so lost, so shattered. How could he have put himself in this position again? To care about someone, knowing it would only make him vulnerable, knowing he'd barely survived the last time, knew he wouldn't be able to do it a second time.

"I'm sorry I've hurt you, that's the last thing I ever wanted to do, but the truth of the matter is, Katie, this shouldn't have happened, can't ever happen again." He paused, took a deep breath and tried to gather his scrambled thoughts. "I don't have anything to offer you." He spread his hands out helplessly. "Absolutely nothing. Not you, not Rusty—"

"Don't bring my son into this," she snapped, furious and hurt. "This is between you and me and has nothing to do with him. And if I recall, you're the one who made the distinction that our professional lives never interfere or overlap into our personal ones. And you can't get much more personal than this. But this is between you and me, Lucas, and has nothing to do with my son or your relationship with him." Closing her eyes, she took a deep breath and tried to gather her composure. But his words had struck like a blow straight to her heart.

She loved him, and yes, now she could honestly admit it, at least to herself. She had love in her heart, and all he had was fear she wanted something from him.

"Katie, listen to me," he all but demanded, raising his voice for the first time in memory. "I don't have anything to offer you. Absolutely nothing. And I'm sorry for it but this doesn't change anything," he said, feeling like a heel and wishing he could take back everything he'd said. But he knew he couldn't. This was best, for both of them. He couldn't afford the feelings growing for her and Rusty. He simply couldn't. They terrified him on a level he couldn't even put a voice to.

"Lucas, just so we're clear here, I don't recall asking for or voicing any expectations to you." She wished her voice was stronger, less strained and teary, but it couldn't be helped.

"Maybe not yet," he said, realizing he was just digging himself in deeper. "Just because we've made love, it doesn't mean anything," he stammered, cursing himself even as he said it. "It doesn't change anything."

Temper erupted, smothering over the hurt. "Doesn't mean anything?" she repeated, her face and voice stricken. "I can't believe you just said that." How could he dismiss something that was so beautiful, so perfect? She had no idea.

She wanted to laugh it off, to show that she was a sophisticated, modern woman who could simply make love with a man and then pretend it didn't matter, didn't touch her heart and her soul, but she couldn't simply because she wasn't that kind of woman. She would never have made love with him if she hadn't loved him. And to simply pretend otherwise would be a lie, something she wasn't keen on doing, not now, not about this, and especially not with him.

She could never deny the importance of what had just happened between them, not even to ease his own conscience.

"I'm very sorry that this meant nothing to you, Lucas. I'm sorry that somehow I've frightened you into thinking that I wanted or expected something more than the beautiful evening we shared together tonight." Sniffling, she wrapped the afghan tighter around her and stood up with the dignity of a queen. "I can assure you I want or expect nothing from you. Not now, not ever."

She was glad the afghan covered her legs so he wouldn't see her knees were knocking—they wouldn't have carried her now except for sheer pride and will. "What we shared tonight was beautiful and special, nothing more, nothing less, and if you regret it I'm sorry for you."

"Katie, wait." He reached for her, knowing he'd blown it, knowing he'd hurt her and not knowing how to fix it and yet still protect himself emotionally.

"Please." She had to swallow the lump in her throat, and the pebble of pain in her heart seemed to have grown to a boulder. "Don't touch me. Not right now," she added more gently, shoving her hair back. "It's late, Lucas. We're both tired. Maybe it would be best if you just…left."

"You want me to leave?" He wanted to beg for her forgiveness, to throw himself at her mercy, to let her know this had nothing to do with her, and everything to do with him. He couldn't afford to feel anything for her, couldn't allow himself to be vulnerable, not ever again. But he knew she'd never understand, not unless he told her the whole truth, and he simply couldn't and he knew it.

"Yes, please," she managed quietly. He nodded.

"I'll just….uh…get my stuff together."

"Do that," she said, wrapping the afghan tighter around her. She clung to her dignity, even as he gathered his things and made his way toward the house to the front door.

"Look, Katie," he said when he reached the door. "I really am sorry."

She managed a weak smile. "There's nothing to be

sorry for, Lucas. Truly." The pain was back in his eyes, making her want to gather him in her arms and hold him until the pain went away. But she couldn't and wouldn't, knowing that he didn't even trust her enough to know that after tonight she wouldn't be wanting or expecting anything from him, except the one thing he couldn't and wouldn't ever offer her: his love.

Before she could protest, he leaned forward and kissed her forehead. "Good night, Katie," he said, before opening the door and stepping out.

"Good night, Lucas." She waited, watching until he was down the stairs before slowing closing the door behind him. The sob she'd been holding back caught her off guard, and Katie leaned against the door as sobs shook her entire body. Unable to stop the tears or the cold that seemed to be seeping deeply into her right to the bones, she sank to the floor, wrapped the afghan tighter around her and let the sobs free.

Chapter Ten

Katie nursed her broken heart and threw herself into her work, but she didn't hear from Lucas. He still saw Rusty almost every day, but he made sure he was gone by the time she got home. He was deliberately avoiding her and there was nothing she could do about it.

Not wanting her relationship, or lack of it, to interfere with her son's relationship with Lucas, Katie tried to put on a brave face, but it was hard, especially when Rusty questioned her about Lucas not hanging around when she was around.

"Did you guys, like, have a fight or something?" Rusty asked on Monday evening, when Lucas hightailed it out of there a scant few minutes before Katie got home.

"A fight?" Katie repeated, carrying a bag of groceries into the kitchen and pretending to be intensely interested in unpacking it. "No, honey, we didn't have a fight." She shrugged, trying to hide the pain she'd been trying to conceal since Lucas left on Saturday. "But remember, Lucas is *your* buddy, it's you he's here to see, not me, remember?" She had to keep reminding herself of that.

"But...are you...like, mad at him or something?" Rusty asked worriedly.

"Honey." Katie set down a can of coffee and turned to her son. "I know you're worried and upset, but please don't be. Lucas and I are still friends, it's just we're both very busy people."

"You're mad," he confirmed with a scowl, making Katie lift his chin.

"Listen, sport, I'm simply busy," she lied. She didn't like lying to him, and in fact, never had, but this was personal, too personal, and she wasn't ready to burden her son with her own stupidity. Besides, as long as Lucas didn't let what happened between them affect his relationship with her son, she wanted to protect Rusty from the truth—if she could. "You know I have a lot of responsibility at the paper, and I really don't have that much time to socialize. Besides," she added, forcing a smile, "this has nothing to do with your relationship with Lucas. That's still fine, isn't it?"

"I guess so," he mumbled, looking totally dejected.

"Good. Then stop worrying and go get washed up for dinner." As soon as Rusty left, she all but collapsed against the counter, blinking back tears. The strain of pretending everything was all right when her heart was breaking was simply getting to be too much for her.

But she had no choice, she wasn't going to worry her son, not about this, ever. It was her own fault for allowing her feelings for Lucas to get out of control.

It had been her decision, now she had to face and accept the consequences. But it would help if she understood this, understood what had happened. Lucas was not a cold man, not at all, but something had happened after they'd made love that had made him seem cold and curt—what, she didn't know. He was frightened, she'd realized belatedly, and she couldn't seem to understand why.

It plagued her all night, making it difficult to concentrate on her work. When Rusty went to bed, she finally realized that she had no way of knowing what had happened since she really had no idea what had happened in Lucas's past. And she had a feeling that was the key to what had frightened him—his past.

She'd promised him she wouldn't pry or dig into his past, at least not in her capacity as the editor of the newspaper or in her role as a reporter. And Lucas was the one who asked her to make certain she kept the two distinctly separate.

And she had.

But this was different, this was *personal*. Very personal. It had nothing to do with her job at the paper and everything to do with her heart. She was in love with the man and she had a right to know what had happened in his past to make him so frightened of her and what they shared together.

She went to her computer, saved the file she'd been working on, closed it and then took a deep breath. She stared at the blank screen for a moment before taking the plunge. She opened another file and typed in Lucas's full name, and then she nervously waited, curious now to find out exactly what Lucas had been hiding from her all along.

By Thursday, Katie had learned that Lucas had been married, but was now widowed. Apparently a lot of his files and records, at least the official ones from his years on the Chicago police force—something else she hadn't even known before—had been sealed at Lucas's request. A judge had granted a court order to seal all Lucas's personnel and personal records from the department, only leading Katie to wonder why. The more she found out, the more questions she had.

She didn't have much time to work on this, but tried to do a little each night, and now had her notebook filled with information and some additional questions she was trying to find answers for.

By Thursday, she still hadn't seen or heard from Lucas, but Rusty called her at the office to ask if he could go to Lucas's lake cabin for the weekend.

"Yeah, Ma," Rusty said excitedly. "Lucas says it's gonna be an all-guy weekend. He invited Sean and his dad to go, and some other guys too. So can I go, huh, can I? We're gonna fish and watch football and really pig out. You know, just do guy stuff."

Not even the joyful exuberance in her son's voice eased her aching heart. Lucas had chosen this weekend deliberately since he knew there was no way she'd be able to go, not when she had such a pressing deadline facing her.

Lucas was sending her a message, loud and clear,

that he'd continue to see Rusty, but he didn't want to see her. It hurt, more than she believed possible, but she'd known better than to allow herself to let her feelings for Lucas get out of hand. And she let it happen anyway and had no one to blame but herself.

"Of course you can go, sweetheart," she said to Rusty, closing her eyes against the pain and trying to make her voice cheerful.

"Uh…Ma?" He hesitated. "Will you…uh…be okay by yourself? I mean, I've never gone away before, and well…left you all alone before…" Rusty's voice trailed.

"I'll be fine, sweetheart," she assured him, blinking back tears. Having Rusty worry about her was a switch, and he'd been doing it all week in spite of her assurances that nothing was wrong. "I've got tons of work to finish and this will give me a chance to dig into it uninterrupted. When you get back, the Halloween issue will be done and we can just enjoy Halloween and the carnival. I want you to go and have a wonderful time."

"And…uh…you're sure you'll…like, be okay?" he asked again, and she smiled.

"I'll be fine, honey. I don't want you worrying about me. Why don't you start getting the stuff together you want to take. Make sure you pack warm clothes, it's going to be cold up at the lake this time of year."

"Yo, Katie, we got a problem," Lindsey yelled from her desk. Katie turned and held up her finger through her office window to let Lindsey know she was on the phone.

"Sweetheart, I'm sorry, I've got to go. I'll be home at the normal time. And just ask Grandma to help you with your stuff if you're not sure what to take, okay?"

"Okay, see you when you get home, Ma. Bye."

Katie hung up the phone and walked into the outer office. "Lindsey, what's wrong now?" she asked, trying to keep the exasperation out of her voice. She was exhausted from being unable to sleep all week, and just plain worn-out from all the work she'd been doing. She could do with a little less drama and a little bit more calm in her life.

"Mayor just called, seems he's called an emergency meeting."

"Oh, for Pete's sake, now what?" Katie demanded, dragging a hand through her hair. "I really don't have time for this."

"Katie." Lindsey looked at her long and hard over her spectacles. "Are you feeling poorly or something? You've been just a might touchy all week."

Katie managed a smile, and felt a rush of guilt. "Sorry, Lindsey, with the Halloween issue dogging my heels and the carnival next weekend, I guess I'm just a bit tired and overwhelmed."

Lindsey nodded, not convinced. "Well, once we get this issue to bed, maybe you need to take a few days off."

The thought made Katie laugh. "I don't think so, Lindsey, not with the election issue, and then the Christmas carnival following on the heels of the Halloween issue. We're going to be swamped from now until the end of the year."

"It's that way every year, Katie. Gotta pace yourself," Lindsey advised, still staring at Katie over her glasses. "From late September until New Year's it's havoc around here, but come January, it'll be so slow we'll be going door to door trying to find some news to print."

Katie laughed, realizing Lindsey was right. Normally she loved this time of year, the hustle and bustle, the preparing for the holidays. This was her first year handling the paper during the holiday season, and broken heart or not, she was not going to let anyone take away her pleasure from finally managing the newspaper.

"Don't know what's up, but the mayor's all in a dither." Lindsey glanced at her watch. "You've got five minutes to get to the chief's office."

"The chief's office?" Panic set in, knowing she'd have to face Lucas in front of the entire town council and not certain she could keep her emotions in check. "Why is the mayor having a meeting at the police chief's office?"

"Why's the sky blue?" Lindsey shrugged. "Who knows what's on the man's mind? Not me, not old enough yet," she said with a confirming nod. "But I imagine you'll find out soon enough."

"Terrific," Katie muttered, grabbing her purse and her notepad from her desk. She walked up to Lindsey and laid a hand on her shoulder, giving it a squeeze. "If I've forgotten to say it this week, Lindsey, thank you for everything. For handling the office, for juggling sixty things at once, and for keeping me on track and never losing your cool even when I lose mine." Katie smiled. "I couldn't run this place without you," she added softly.

"Know that," Lindsey said with a nod. "That's why I stay. That, and of course the big bucks you pay me," she added with a smile. "Now get to your meeting so I can close this dang office up for the day. And don't forget since you're going to be working at home tomorrow, I'm not coming in, either. Everyone knows we close on the Friday before the Halloween carnival, but I posted a notice on the front door just in case."

"You enjoy your day off, Lindsey, and have a good weekend," Katie said as she headed out the door.

"Oh, I intend to." Lindsey grinned. "Intend to, indeed."

Lucas's office door was shut, which was odd, Katie thought nervously, as his assistant simply waved her through. Katie took a deep breath, knocked on the door then let herself in.

Lucas, the mayor, and Lucas's two full-time deputies were seated around the round conference table in the corner.

"Katherine," the mayor said, getting up to greet her. "I'm sorry about the late notice, but we've got ourselves a problem here."

"What's wrong?" she asked immediately, taking the empty chair next to the mayor and sinking into it. She laid her notepad on the table and glanced at the assembled group. When she looked at Lucas, her heart tumbled over and began to ache, but if he was unnerved by her presence, he didn't show it. He looked absolutely normal to her, not bothering to give her more than a professional cursory nod and a glance.

"Katie," the mayor began. "We asked you here because we need to know how to handle this situation as far as the newspaper goes. We…uh…don't want to alarm people, but we do want them to be extra careful."

"Mayor, what on earth is going on?" Her glance went from the mayor to Lucas, then back again.

"Katie," Lucas began. "We've had what appears to be two home invasions in town the past week," Lucas stated simply.

"What!" Shock had her voice rising. "Home invasions?" She shook her head. Crime was virtually nonexistent in this town. "I don't understand. In Cooper's Cove?" She glanced at the mayor and he nodded.

"Afraid so, Katie," the mayor said with a sigh and a sad shake of his head. "First one was on Tuesday, and the second one was just yesterday." He sighed. "Thought the first was maybe a mistake, or an isolated incident, but I'm afraid it looks to be more now with this second one."

"Nothing's been taken or vandalized," Lucas informed the group. "And yet whoever is doing this is being deliberate, making certain they rearrange a few things so that the owners know that someone's been in their house."

"But why?" Katie asked, confused. "Why on earth would someone break into a house, rearrange things, but not take anything?" She shook her head. "This doesn't make sense."

"I know." Lucas shuffled through the police reports on his desk. "Funny thing is, every home that's been entered hasn't been locked. So technically they're not breaking in, but merely walking in."

"That's not unusual, Lucas," Katie said, forcing herself to look at him and hold onto her professional stance. Hadn't he been the one to tell her that they had to keep their personal relationship from their professional one? Or rather that whatever happened privately could never affect them in their professional capacity. She wasn't here as Rusty's mom, or Lucas's lover, but as the editor of the newspaper, and as such, she intended to be totally calm and professional—even if it killed her. "No one locks their doors in Cooper's Cove, I certainly never have."

"Well, maybe you'd better," Lucas said more sternly then he intended, looking directly at her. He didn't mean to sound so gruff, but the idea of Katie and Rusty being alone, and with their doors not even locked, worried him deeply.

The mayor cleared his throat, sensing the tension between Katie and Lucas. "Now, with the Halloween carnival next weekend, I don't want to panic people, but, Katie, we were thinking that until we get to the bottom of this, maybe you could run something in the paper. We want to keep the actual incidents to just the people in this room, but we'd like to put out some kind of a message from the chief, here, telling people—"

"Reminding people," Lucas corrected. "To lock their doors at all times, especially when they go out. I'd couch it as just a friendly reminder from the new chief that during this busy holiday season people should take extra precautions and make certain their doors and windows are locked at all times, especially when they leave the house." Lucas frowned in thought. "I'd also add that garage doors leading into houses should be locked and checked as well."

The mayor frowned. "The Halloween carnival is a very popular activity, and folks from other towns usually patronize the carnival. It's one of the biggest moneymakers of the year for the town, so we don't want to scare people away, Katie, nor do we want to alarm anyone in town, but we do want folks to be sensible."

"And careful," Lucas added. He shuffled through his notes again. "My department is on top of this, and we're investigating numerous leads, but until we catch whoever's doing this, precautions are going to be necessary."

"Lucas, do you want to write something up for the paper?" Katie asked, glancing up at him. "I can edit it and get it in when I turn the final blue lines in Saturday afternoon."

"Actually, Katie, I was hoping you might be able to do it since you know so much more about writing and the town." He smiled at her. "If I have to write it, the carnival might be over before I find the right words. That is," he added softly, "if you don't mind."

She shook her head, refusing to let her gaze hold his. "No, of course not, that's my job." She grabbed her notepad and began making notes, not wanting to have to look directly at Lucas. It was too hard and too painful, and she didn't want anyone else to know how deeply upset she really was. "I can get something together and have it put on the front page of the Halloween edition." She glanced up. "Is that all right with everyone?" The group exchanged glances and nodded. "Fine, I'll get right on it."

"Now, I'm going to be gone for the weekend," Lucas informed the group. "I was going to cancel, but the mayor insisted I go."

"Senseless not to, Lucas," the mayor said with a smile, giving him a pat on the shoulder. "You got an assistant chief and two full-time deputies on duty 24/7, so there's no point in you canceling your plans. We can handle things here, can't we, boys?" the mayor asked, looking directly at the assembled deputies, who all nodded. "So you go on and take those boys up to the cabin like you promised. I think if you canceled at this late date it would arouse suspicion and we don't want to do that."

"You're right," Lucas agreed with a nod. "But I'm only an hour and a phone call away," he reminded everyone, glancing around the table. "So we're agreed then that Katie will write up something for the newspaper—"

"Lucas, what about if I print extra copies of what I write up and ask the shops along Main Street to post them in their windows? That way, the notice can be out and up before the end of this weekend instead of waiting until next weekend when the Halloween issue comes out?"

The mayor and Lucas exchanged glances. "That's a great idea, Katie," Lucas said with a smile.

"I'll get something written up before I go home tonight and drop it off with your assistant for your approval. Then I'll have them printed and distributed before the weekend's up. Is that acceptable to everyone?"

Lucas and the mayor nodded. "As long as you're here, Katie, why don't we just work on something now. That way I can give it to one of the boys to have printed up and distributed and it might save some time."

"Sounds like a plan to me," the mayor agreed and Katie almost groaned. The last thing she wanted to do was sit in Lucas's office and try to concentrate, especially with him hovering overhead.

The mayor pushed back from his chair, satisfied his portion of the meeting was finished. "So as long as everyone understands what they're supposed to do and just what the situation is, I think I'll let everyone else all go home to your dinner. Thanks for coming, especially on such short notice. And Katherine, thank you for your help."

Dismissed, the mayor and Lucas's deputies all but fled, leaving Katie and Lucas alone.

Nervous, and aware he was watching her, Katie absently flipped through her notebook looking for a blank page.

"Katie."

Her hands froze and she looked up at him. "Yes?" she said in her best professional voice.

"How are you?" he asked quietly, aching to reach across the table to touch her. She looked so tired and weary, he wanted to just drag her into his arms and hold her.

"Busy," she said coolly. "So I'd like to get this done as quickly as possible because I still have a lot of work to do today."

He nodded. "Fine." He glanced over at her notepad. "I noticed you started writing something while the mayor was still talking. Mind if I take a look?"

She pushed her notepad across the table from him. "Be my guest."

He flipped a couple of pages and too late she realized the notes she'd been taking on his past, the information she'd been trying to assemble was all right there, in her notebook.

She knew the moment he found the information. He flipped a page over and saw his name at the top of a page.

Lucas's hand stilled and his head came up slowly. "Have you been spying on me?" His voice was as cold as his eyes.

"No, Lucas, I wasn't spying. It wasn't like that." Desperate, she dragged a hand through her hair as he began flipping through her notes on him. "Please, listen to me," she demanded desperately. "I'll admit I was trying to find out some information about your background, and your past, but not as a reporter, never as a reporter," she assured him. "But as a woman. A woman who cares very much about you." She hated the look in his eyes. It was as cold and sharp as an icicle and threatened to cut her to the quick.

Lucas slammed her notepad to the table. "Do you really expect me to believe that? Believe you?" His voice was so low and controlled it sent shivers racing through her. "You're a reporter, Katie, remember? Everything is fodder for a hot story, isn't it?" He pushed his chair back and stood up, stalking the office in a fury. "I trusted you, Katie, because you gave me your word. And you broke it. I should have known better. Once a reporter, always a reporter. You reporters think it's perfectly acceptable to dig into people's lives and pasts without regard for anyone else's feelings or emotions. All you care about is your stories, your precious stories. I thought you were different, I thought I could trust you. Now I see how wrong I was."

"No, Lucas, wait, it's not like that." She reached out to him, but he ignored her. "Please, listen to me." Tears clogged her throat, her voice—the last thing she wanted to do was make the situation with him worse.

"Why? So you can tell me some more lies?" He turned to her, his face a frigid mask. "Drop off the information with my assistant when it's finished," he said. "I'm going to dinner. Shut the door on your way out."

He stormed out of his office, leaving Katie stunned and staring after him.

Heartsick and not knowing what to do about it, Katie wrote up the short article reminding everyone to start locking their doors and windows, and dropped it off with Lucas's assistant before finally going home.

She was both exhausted and heartsick, but she still had to make dinner, and help Rusty get packed for his trip.

Long after Rusty went to sleep she was still in her home office, working on edits, trying to concentrate.

Around eleven, unable to concentrate any longer, she pulled off her reading glasses, rubbed her eyes, then glanced out the window.

She jumped up the moment she spotted Lucas get out of his car. She didn't know what he was doing here, but she was grateful. She wasn't comfortable with the way things had ended in his office this afternoon. Not loving her or not wanting a relationship with her was one thing, but thinking she was unscrupulous was quite another. And she didn't deserve it.

She hurried to the front door so the bell wouldn't wake Rusty, and pulled it open just before Lucas reached for the bell.

"Hi," she said quietly, drinking in the sight of him.

"Can we talk for a minute?" he asked and she nodded. His face was drawn and pale, and he looked awful.

Her heart ached just looking at him and she simply wanted to pull him into her arms and comfort him.

"Would you like to come in?" she asked and he nodded, stepping through the door.

She pulled her robe tighter as she walked back to the family room, suddenly feeling self-conscious, which was ridiculous considering what had happened between them. But she wouldn't think about that now, wouldn't make any prejudgments about what he wanted to talk about. She'd simply listen.

"Can I get you anything?" she asked quietly, mindful that Rusty was sleeping just down the hall. He shook his head, but he didn't sit, merely paced in front of her.

"I came to apologize for this afternoon. I was wrong, Katie, and I realize now that you had every right to know about the man who's so involved in your son's life. And in yours," he added softly. "If the situation was reversed I'm sure I'd feel the same way. I don't know how much you've discovered on your own—"

"Not much," she said quietly. "All of your records have been sealed, Lucas. But I'm sure you're aware of that."

He nodded and continued pacing, slipping his trembling hands in his pockets. "That's normal whenever there's a murder involving a cop's family."

"Murder?" Shock had her all but gaping at him. Of all the things she'd imagined, this wasn't one of them.

"Katie, I was a Chicago cop for seventeen years. I worked primarily undercover in the gang crimes unit. I was very close to bringing down a major gang leader who was responsible for bringing tons of drugs into the country, drugs that were flooding the streets of Chicago, hooking and killing our kids. I'd been working on this particular case for almost two years. I was married and had a son. His name was Todd and he was just a little bit older than Rusty is right now. My wife hated my work, hated that I was a cop. She wanted me to give it up and go into her father's business. I refused." He took a deep breath. "I won't pretend my marriage was perfect. Far, far from it. And I don't believe in divorce, especially when a child is involved, but my wife refused to have any more children as long as I was a cop. I refused to give up my career, so there you have it. A stalemate. Two people who were making each other seriously unhappy for no reason other than they both wanted their own way."

Katie tucked her knees under her, suddenly cold as he continued to pace. She remembered the night he'd asked her about giving up her dreams. Now she understood what he meant. His wife had wanted him to give up his dream of being a cop.

"I'm sorry, Lucas," she said quietly, not certain what else to say.

"A little over two years ago, unbeknownst to me, my cover was blown. The drug dealer I'd been after had a snitch, someone who also worked with the department and ratted me out. I didn't know it until after…"

"After?" she prompted softly, seeing the pain and grief on his face.

"One morning, we all overslept. It was a bitterly cold Chicago day and my wife couldn't get her car started to drive my son to school, so she took mine. The drug dealer had planted a bomb in my car, a bomb meant to kill me." He couldn't look at her. "It killed my wife and son instead."

"Oh, God, Lucas." She was on her feet, going to him, wrapping her arms around him, holding his stiff body. "I'm sorry. I'm so sorry." Tears filled her eyes, spilled over. She couldn't even begin to imagine the grief of losing both your spouse and your only child. "I can't even imagine what you've been through."

He stepped back and away from her, holding up a shaky hand. "Katie, please let me finish or I might not be able to."

She nodded and sat down again.

"The press had a field day. The murders of a cop's family is big news. The entire police force was on the hunt for the killer, and of course each day every reporter in town was scratching for the latest tidbit or update of news. They hounded me and one day followed me and my partner to a stakeout and blew our cover. This reporter almost got my partner killed. I finally had to resign from the force just to get away from the reporters because I simply couldn't be responsible for someone else's life, not ever again. Can you understand, that?"

"Can I understand that you wanted, needed and deserved some peace to grieve for your family in private—of course. I understand that there would be a certain amount of guilt on your part, just like the guilt I had when Jed died. But, Lucas, you weren't responsible. You didn't plant that bomb."

"The hell I wasn't responsible. If I had given up the

police force like my wife wanted she and my son would still be alive."

"You don't know that, Lucas. You can't, not for sure. You can't say what might have been. We can only live with what is, and I understand how you must have felt. Remember, I've been there. I lost my spouse, too. But Lucas, things happen that we have no control over. And we simply can't take or accept responsibility for other people's actions. We can only take and accept responsibility for our own." Katie was quiet for a moment, her mind spinning to put the pieces together finally. "That's why you hate reporters?" she said with a nod. "Now it makes sense. That's why the first night we met you accused me of spying on you."

"Yeah." Lucas sighed and finally sank down into the recliner next to the fireplace. He didn't trust himself to sit next to Katie, to be close to her, to smell her scent, her body heat, knowing he might not be able to control himself, and he had to hold onto his control. It was all he had left at this point.

"I'm sorry, Lucas, truly and deeply sorry. I can't even imagine how you go on after losing a child." She shook her head, blinked back tears, her own pain for him searing through her at the unimaginable loss.

His smile was raw, his face ravaged by grief. "You know, that's the one question I got asked probably more than anything. How do you get up in the morning knowing you've lost a child?" He surged to his feet. "How the hell am I supposed to answer that? Do I tell people that losing your child is like having someone reach into your heart and rip it out? That the hole inside of you just seems to grow and fester until all you can feel is the pain and emptiness, each and every second of every day that you're alive and your child isn't. It's a constant reminder that you've lost your child. That you'll never see his face again. Or hear his laughter. Or throw a ball with him. Or hug him tight." He had to swallow, the knot in his throat was the size of a baseball and almost choking him. "Do you know what's it's like to know your son will never see another birthday or Christmas or another first snow? How do you explain that to someone? How can you explain that you'll never dance at your son's wedding, or kiss your first grandchild? How can you explain the pain that comprises every second of your life, pain unlike anything anyone has ever experienced? Pain that there is no explanation for, and yet everyone expects you to just go on living, day by day as if you're normal. Katie, I'll never be normal again. Is that what I'm supposed to say? Hell, I just don't know anymore. How the hell am I supposed to live with the guilt of knowing I'm responsible for my only son's death? I'm alive and he's not, and God, I'd trade places with him in an instant. If I could only have him back for just a few more moments." His voice broke and he turned away from her trying to garner some control.

Drained, and fearing the last of his control was slipping, Lucas rubbed his tearing eyes before turning back to her. "That's why I told you I don't have anything to offer you or Rusty, Katie. Because I don't. My heart is empty," he admitted. "Frozen over. And there's nothing I can do about it."

"Lucas—"

"No, listen to me!" He held up his hand to stop her words. "I will never again put anyone else's life at risk by loving them. Not ever again. Do you understand me? Do you understand what I'm saying? If anything ever happened, I simply couldn't handle it. Not again. Not ever again. The loss almost killed me the first time, I won't survive it a second time."

"Lucas." Katie got to her feet and went to him, wrapping her arms around his stiff body, refusing to let him push her away. Love overflowed in her heart, and she wasn't certain how he couldn't see it, feel it. "Lucas, please don't," she whispered, laying her head on his chest. "Please don't say you can't love again. You'll be cheating yourself as well as us. We love you, Lucas." Her voice broke as the tears came harder. "Rusty and I both love you." And she knew as she spoke it, it was the truth.

"No, Katie, don't—please. Don't love me because I can't return that love. I can't risk it." His voice shuddered out. Her scent, her touch was unraveling him, and he wrapped his arms around her and simply held on, savoring this last embrace, knowing he could never have what he wanted and needed most. "I'm sorry, Katie," he whispered against her hair. "I'm truly sorry." Afraid the dam of control was going to break, Lucas dropped his arms, and turned, fleeing through the house and out the door.

Stunned and shaken, Katie curled up on the couch and wept for herself, for Rusty and more importantly, for Lucas.

* * *

On Friday, Lucas didn't bother to come to the door, he merely beeped his horn and Rusty, who'd been ready and waiting since he'd come home from school, raced out the door to meet him.

Katie had no idea how to handle this situation with Lucas. None at all, so for now, she was going to do what she had to—her edits. It was the only thing she could do if she wanted to keep her sanity.

This whole situation with Lucas was such a mess, she had no idea how they'd ever make things right again. Or if they even could. She could probably accept that he didn't love her—wouldn't let himself love her. Eventually, she rationalized.

But her heart was so heavy, her spirits so low, she couldn't wait to get done with her work so she could just have some time to settle down and try to think her way out of this mess.

On Saturday, she worked at home until the edits were finished, then drove them over to the printer.

Exhausted, but relieved that the enormous Halloween issue had finally been put to bed, Katie decided that since she had a free evening, with no chores, no responsibilities, and no child to tend to, she was going to simply relax for one night. She simply didn't have the energy for anything else.

On the way home from the printer she stopped at the video store and rented a couple of old movies, then headed home with plans to do nothing more strenuous than taking a hot bubble bath.

She hadn't eaten much in the past week. She'd been

too upset. About the only thing she could stomach right now was the idea of popcorn, so she planned to make some and have it for dinner.

By the time she finally got home and took her bath, it was dark out. It was so eerily quiet in the house, she hadn't counted on the loneliness that set in, only making her heart ache more. Funny, all the years she and Rusty were alone she'd been far too busy to be lonely, and in fact, had never really thought about it.

But now, with Rusty away and Lucas out of her life—probably forever—she found that the unbearable ache of loneliness crept up on her, settling in and spoiling her mood.

After her bath, she pulled on warm pajamas and a robe, lit a fire in the fireplace, then headed to the kitchen to pop some popcorn. She'd just pulled the pot off the stove when the doorbell rang.

Frowning at the clock, Katie tightened the sash on her robe and went to the door, wondering who on earth was paying a visit at almost eight on a Saturday night.

She pulled open the door, surprised to see her mother and her aunt huddled together against the night's chill.

"Katherine, dear," her mother began worriedly as the chilly night wind swirled around her. "We saw the signs posted in town—"

"Yes, dear, the note from Lucas reminding everyone to lock their doors," her aunt injected.

"And we knew we had to come talk to you," her mother finished in a rush.

"Well, come in out of the cold," Katie said, pulling

them both in. "I was just making some popcorn, and I lit a fire in the fireplace, so come on back to the family room and warm up, and then we'll talk." Katie made her way to the back of the house where the smell of fresh popcorn filled the air.

"Oh, it smells so good in here," Louella said, unwrapping her scarf and slipping off her coat.

"And the fire's nice," Gracie said with a smile, taking her coat off as well.

"Can I get you something to drink? Some coffee?"

"No, dear," her mother said, sinking down on the couch and waving Katie's offer away. "I just need to sit a moment." She pressed a hand to her heart, immediately alarming Katie.

"Mama, what's wrong? What's got you so upset?" She sat next to her mother and took her hand. Her mother smiled and patted Katie's hand in return.

"Maybe I'd better let Gracie explain," Louella said vaguely. Katie turned to her aunt, who was sitting in the old recliner next to the fireplace.

"Katie, dear, you know sometimes things aren't exactly as they seem," her aunt began mysteriously, and Katie nodded.

"Okay," she said slowly. "I understand that." What she didn't understand was what they were both so upset about. "Sometimes things aren't as they seem. Got it."

"Especially with the males in our life," Gracie went on, only confusing Katie more.

"The big and little…males, dear," her mother added, exchanging a glance with her sister. "And dear, we don't want you worrying unnecessarily," she added, and Katie laughed.

"Too late for that, Mama. I started worrying the minute I had Rusty." She looked at her mother carefully. "Does this have something to do with Rusty?"

"In a way, dear, yes." Her mother sighed. "I don't know how to explain exactly what's in your astrological charts, dear, or in Rusty's, but remember when I told you that you were going to face some trying times this month?"

"Of yeah, I remember," Katie said, considering what had happened with Lucas, how could she forget.

"Well, dear, those trying times aren't quite over yet, and we didn't want you to be unduly upset."

"About what?" Katie asked, and her mom and aunt exchanged glances again.

"About everything that's going on, dear. With Rusty and Lucas," Gracie added knowingly. "And of course, you'll want to buy a wedding present."

Katie merely blinked at her aunt, then she sighed and held up her hand. "Okay, let's take this one thing at a time, Aunt Gracie. Why do I want to buy a wedding present? And for who?"

"Why, for Lindsey," her aunt said as if it was perfectly clear.

"Lindsey?" Katie repeated, shocked. "Are you telling me that Lindsey's getting married?" Katie looked at her mother, then back at her aunt. "How come I'm the last one to know?"

"Well, dear," Gracie went on, patting her pearls, "normally when you elope you don't tell anyone, I mean, isn't that the point? You keep it a secret." She looked at her sister for confirmation and Louella nodded in total agreement.

"Aunt Gracie, *when* is Lindsey getting married?" Katie was having a very hard time taking in all of this.

"*Got* married, dear," her aunt corrected with a smile. "Today. She and Mr. Hensen eloped. But don't worry, I'm sure she'll be back in the office bright and early on Monday morning." Gracie's smile widened and her eyes glazed a bit. "In fact, I know it."

Katie pressed a hand to her forehead, trying to digest this. The headache that had been plaguing her was getting stronger. "And you're sure you're talking about my Lindsey?" she asked, wanting to be absolutely clear. "The one who's worked at the paper for…forever?"

"Yes, dear, that Lindsey. There isn't another one in town, is there?" Gracie asked with a slight frown and Katie shook her head.

"Not that I know of."

Suddenly Gracie beamed and clapped her hands together. "And she made a beautiful bride, Katie, just beautiful." Her aunt sighed dreamily. "It's a shame she kept the ceremony such a secret. Why, neither of them told a soul, not a soul."

Katie blew out a breath. "If it was a secret, Aunt Gracie, and neither of them told a soul, how on earth did you find—" Katie broke off when her aunt merely lifted a brow and smiled serenely. "Okay, scratch that, I don't think I want to know how you knew." Katie blew out another breath. "Okay, so Lindsey and Mr. Hensen eloped this weekend. I'll make a note to buy them a wedding present." She turned to her mother again. "Now, Mama, please tell me what all this has to do with Rusty? And why you're so upset."

"Well, dear, your aunt believes—"

"Katie dear, after we saw the signs in town, we knew we had to come talk to you. There's not really a crime wave going on in town—"

"Aunt Gracie, how…how did you know?" She simply stared at her aunt in shock. "No one but Lucas, the mayor, me and Lucas's deputies know about what happened in town. And the signs merely reminded people to lock their doors and windows. They didn't say anything about what's already happened."

"Yes, dear, I know, and normally I wouldn't say something like this, but because it might involve…Rusty…now don't get upset, Katie, it's not what you think."

"Wait a minute." Katie got up to pace, her nerves jangling in alarm. "Are you saying these mysterious break-ins in town have something to do with Rusty?"

"Well, yes and no, dear," Gracie said.

"Remember, things aren't always as they seem, dear," her mother reminded her.

"Okay, enough," Katie said, raising her hands in the air. "Someone please tell me what's going on before I scream."

"Now dear, please don't get upset," her mother admonished.

"Too late, Mama. Now someone spill it," she demanded, glancing from her mom to her aunt. "If this involves Rusty, then I need to know."

"Well, dear, Rusty's not alone in this," Gracie said.

"Sean?" Katie asked with a lift of her brow, knowing Rusty never did anything without Sean.

Her aunt nodded. "I'm afraid so, dear. Apparently the boys thought if…well…if there were some mysterious goings-on in town, that would force you and Lucas together—"

"Because you write the 'Police Beat' column, dear," her mother interjected with a weak smile.

"And that maybe then you and Lucas would become more than friends, and you could be a family."

Stunned, Katie dragged a hand through her hair and continued pacing, much as Lucas had just a couple of nights before. "Oh, God, I can't believe that kid thought that by breaking into houses, committing a criminal act, it would draw Lucas and I together."

"He wants a father, dear," her mother said softly. "Like the other boys." Her mother shrugged. "I don't imagine this comes as much of a surprise."

"Surprise?" Katie laughed but the sound held no humor. "Mama, I'm shocked. What on earth was he thinking?"

"He wasn't thinking, dear," Gracie said calmly. "And Katie, he technically didn't break in anywhere. He only went into houses that weren't locked."

"How on earth did you—" Katie shook her head. "Never mind, Aunt Gracie, I don't want to know. And you're sure about this? All of it?"

"Well, certainly dear," Gracie said. "I wouldn't be here otherwise."

"Okay, I'll take care of this tomorrow as soon as Rusty gets home."

"Now, dear, we don't want you to be upset," her mother said.

"Well, Mama, it's too late because I'm really upset."

"You didn't fail, Katie dear," Gracie said gently. "And there's no point in thinking that way. Rusty is just a typical boy who wants what he's never had. That's not such a bad thing. He just went about getting it the wrong way." Gracie smiled. "But like I said, everything's going to work out in the end. Truly, dear, so don't worry." Her aunt stood up, smoothed down her caftan, then smiled. "We'd better go, your mother has a date with the mayor."

Katie turned to her mother. "Mama, did you and Mayor Hannity…make up?"

Her mother smiled. "Let's just say Harry saw the error of his ways."

"Is that why you decided not to run for mayor?" Katie asked suspiciously. Her mother had called her earlier in the week and told her not to bother holding out two pages for her in the newspaper since she wasn't going to run for mayor after all.

"Yes, I guess you could say so," her mother commented vaguely, standing and reaching for her coat. Katie went over and helped her with it. "Sometimes the men in our lives just need a gentle jolt, something to make them appreciate us." Her mother's smile was serene. "I don't think Harry will take me for granted or put his job ahead of me again, do you, Gracie?"

Gracie chuckled as she slipped her coat on. "No, Louella, I honestly don't."

"And are you happy about this, Mama?" Katie asked, wanting at least someone in her family to be happy.

"Oh, dear, yes," Louella said. "I was merely trying to prove a point to the hardheaded man. I never intended to really become mayor, dear. I merely let it be known that I was going to run for mayor." Her mother winked. "They are definitely two distinctly separate things. I knew that would put the fear of God into the man, and it did." Her mother nodded. "Proved my point, too."

"Yes, you did," Gracie said, slipping her own coat on. "Now, Katie, dear, we're sorry we just barged in on you. Try to relax and let us know what happens with Rusty."

"Oh, I will," Katie promised as she followed her mom and aunt to the door and pulled it open. "Stay warm," she said, giving them both a kiss good night.

Gracie stopped on the stoop and turned back to Katie. "Dear, you'll have plenty of time to get the Fourth of July issue out, so don't fret about it. And Savannah's a beautiful name for a little girl, don't you think?" With a serene smile and no further explanation, her aunt waved at her. "Good night, dear."

"'Night." Katie slowly closed the door. Then leaned against it and closed her eyes, rubbing her throbbing temples. She couldn't handle one more thing tonight, not one more. But her aunt's words kept reverberating in her ear.

July.

A little girl named Savannah.

Oh God, just for tonight Katie wasn't going to think about what her aunt said—the possibility she might be pregnant—until tomorrow.

* * *

Katie was waiting on the front porch when Lucas pulled into the driveway with Rusty. She was determined not to miss Lucas.

When they spotted her, they both grinned and waved. She walked to the car as Rusty got out, and Lucas rolled down his window.

"Lucas, I'm sorry to ask, but can you come in for a minute?" Sensing he was about to refuse, she hurried on. "I've got some information on the home invasions I think you need to hear."

"Sure," he said. "I'll be right in."

Katie followed behind Rusty, struggling mightily to hold onto her temper.

"Did you have a good time, honey?" she asked, forcing herself to behave normally as he bounded up the front stairs with his sleeping bag and clothes.

"Awesome," he said with a roll of his eyes. "Just awesome."

"Good. I want you to go put your stuff away and then meet me in the family room."

"Why?" he asked, turning back to her, suddenly feeling jittery by the tone of her voice and the look on her face.

"Family meeting," she informed him, and the mere mention of a family meeting had him hurrying through the house and to his room to put away his stuff.

She went into the family room to pace. Nerves kept her from staying still. When she heard the front door close, she knew Lucas had come in.

"Lucas, I'm back here," she called, and a moment later he walked into the family room.

"What's up?" he asked. "Did something happen while I was gone?" He was certain his deputies would have called him, and if they hadn't someone's head was going to roll.

"Have a seat, Lucas, and I'm sure Rusty will explain everything."

"Ma, you…uh…wanted…to see…me?" Rusty, looking nervous and scared, hovered in the doorway, trying not to fidget.

"Come on in, Rusty. I think you have something to tell Lucas?"

"I do?" he said in surprise. His steps slowed when he saw his mother's brow lift. The only time she looked like that was when he was in trouble. Big trouble. Still, he couldn't resist asking. "Am I in trouble or something, Ma?"

"Or something," she snapped, leaning against the fireplace. "Now, Rusty, I want you to tell Lucas exactly what you and Sean have been up to. And I want you to tell him everything."

Rusty's face paled. "Everything?" His voice squeaked upward and he flushed, looking from his mother to Lucas and then down at his shoes.

"Oh, yeah, every single thing. From the beginning."

"Katie, I don't understand—"

"You will," Katie assured him. "Just listen to what Rusty has to say."

"Uh…Lucas, me and Sean…well, we both think…actually all the guys think you're really awesome." Rusty swallowed hard. "And so I was just…uh…wondering what it would be like to have you for a…you know…dad."

"A dad?" Lucas repeated, stunned. He had no idea Rusty felt that way about him. His own heart, filled with feelings for the boy, began to ache.

"Yeah, a dad. *My* dad," Rusty clarified, staring hard at the toe of his sneaker, unable to look at Lucas. "But my ma said you guys were just…friends, so me and Sean figured if we did something…you know…something that would…kinda force you two to spend more time together, that maybe you'd like each other as more than friends, and that maybe then you'd want to be…like…my dad."

Touched but confused, Lucas kept his gaze on Rusty's. "I understand everything you've said, Rusty, and I'm honored, truly, but I don't understand what this has to do with—"

"Tell him, Rusty," Katie prompted, going to her son and putting her arm around him for support even though she was so furious with him she wanted to ground him until he was forty.

"Me and…Sean…we…uh…went into a couple of houses in town." He rushed on at the look on Lucas's face. "We didn't mean any harm, but we thought if you thought someone was breaking into places, then you'd have to meet with my mom, you know because of her 'Police Beat' column, and then we figured you'd have to spend more time together, and I knew if you just spent more time with her, you'd love her, like…like I do."

Lucas's eyes slid closed for a moment, just a brief moment as his heart nearly burst with love, and he took a deep breath before opening his eyes, and his arms.

"Come here, son," he said to Rusty, who shuffled slowly over to Lucas who wrapped his arms around him.

How could he not love this boy? This boy who'd wanted nothing more than what he himself had always wanted—the dream of his life—to have someone who loved him, wanted him. Not to replace the child he'd lost, nothing could ever do that, but there was no reason he couldn't find the love in his heart to share with another child, another boy who loved and needed him.

And this child wanted him. *Him.* It both humbled and shamed him that he'd been so blinded by his own pain, he couldn't see the boy's.

"I'm…sorry," Rusty sobbed, burying his face in Lucas's shoulder. "We didn't mean to do anything bad. I just wanted a father, that's all. I never had one, not really…and I…I…just really wanted you to be my dad."

Lucas held him and rocked him, saying nothing, his gaze closed so Katie couldn't see what he was thinking or feeling.

When Rusty's sobs subsided, Lucas lifted the boy's shirttail and wiped his face for him, earning a grin because he knew his mother would have a fit about him using his shirt for a tissue.

"I want you to listen to me, Rusty," Lucas said, pulling the boy on his lap, keeping his arms around him. "What you and Sean did was wrong. Very wrong."

"I…know," Rusty said, hanging his head. "But we didn't think anyone would get this upset."

"Rusty, you always have to think about everything you do. You have to think about the consequences. And you didn't in this case. What would you have done if someone was home when you went into those houses? And what if they had a gun?"

"A gun?" Rusty's face went pale. "Jeez, I never thought about that," he said, shivering.

"That's right. You didn't think, and as much as I understand your intentions were good, that's never enough. You always have to think of the consequences of every single decision. One wrong or bad decision could have changed your life forever."

"You mean if we went in someone's house and they had a gun and got scared and maybe…like…shot at us?"

"Or shot you," Lucas said calmly and felt the responding tremor in the boy. Clearly this wasn't something the boys had thought about. "Rusty, I want you to promise me right now, give me your solemn oath that you will never, ever do anything like this again. And I want your promise that you will never knowingly do something you know in your heart is wrong just because someone else encourages you to." He pointed to the boy's chest. "You are the only one who's responsible for your actions, do you understand that? You must take and accept responsibility for everything you do, right or wrong. Now, do I have your solemn promise?"

Sniffling, Rusty swiped his nose on his arm and nodded. "Yeah, I promise."

"Good." Lucas nodded. "And I also want you to promise me that you will never again do anything or make a decision without thinking it through clearly so that you know all the consequences. Do you promise?"

"Yeah, I guess so."

"And finally, I want your promise that you will never ever do anything that you know is illegal. Do you promise me?"

Rusty's head nodded up and down. "I promise," he said glumly.

"Good." Lucas patted his back. "I mean think about how it would look if the police chief's son was a juvenile delinquent. That wouldn't be good for my reputation, now would it?"

"Nah…" Rusty said, then wild hope leapt into his eyes and that jittery feeling was back in his stomach. "Son?" he repeated, stunned. "You…uh…want me to be your son?"

"If you'll have me." Lucas held out his other arm. "That is if you and your mother will have me. You see, Rusty, if you would have asked me, I would have told you I didn't have to spend any more time with your mom to love her." His gaze met Katie's as she came to him, joy on her face, tears in her eyes. "You see, I love your mother already, more than anything. And I love you, too, son."

Tears filled Rusty's eyes again and he brushed them off his face. "I…uh…love you, too, Lucas."

Katie sniffled, kissed her son's head, then bent to kiss Lucas. "I love you," she whispered, and he grinned.

"And I love you, both of you." Lucas closed his eyes and felt something fill his empty, aching heart. Love. Sweet and pure. It filled up the hole to almost overflowing, and he grabbed both Rusty and Katie tightly. "I love you both so much."

"Uh…Lucas," Rusty said, drawing back a bit. "Am I like…gonna be punished…or something?"

Katie and Lucas exchanged looks, then grins.

"Oh, yeah, son, definitely," Lucas confirmed. "It's called taking responsibility for your actions."

"Are you...like going to tell...Sean's parents?" Rusty asked nervously, then heaved a sigh of relief when Lucas shook his head.

"No, son, I'm not going to tell them. You are." Lucas released Rusty and grabbed Katie's hand. "Right now. We're going over to Sean's house, and then I think we need to go have a family dinner so we can discuss our wedding. Then we'll discuss your punishment."

"Cow cakes," Rusty muttered, wiping his face again.

Later that night, after Rusty was sound asleep, Katie and Lucas sat snuggled on the couch together. "Lucas," she asked, snuggling closer to him. "Are you sure about this? I mean about...us?" Her heart was so full, but she had to be certain, had to know that his own fears had been calmed.

He reached for her hand, kissed the tip of her fingers. "Sure?" He smiled. "I've never been more sure of anything in my life." He hesitated. "Katie, sometimes life doesn't turn out quite like we planned. That doesn't mean we still can't have all the things that really matter to us, if we work at them. And forgive," he added softly, remembering what Miss Gracie had said about it being time to forgive himself. "I blamed myself for my family's death. I'm sure it's natural, but someone very smart and sweet once told me I deserved to be happy. That my family would have wanted me to be happy." He grinned and kissed her fingertips again, tugging her closer. "And she was right although at the time I didn't believe it. Now I do," he added softly, looking into her eyes. "Love means simply opening your heart, and taking a chance and not being afraid to let yourself love someone else. Tonight, when Rusty was explaining his antics to me, I realized that I could have all the things I really wanted in life, love, a family, and all I had to do was forgive myself and open my heart. And you and Rusty have filled it. Totally." He looked at her carefully. "Now what about you? Are you sure about this? About us?"

She chuckled. "Lucas, I've never been more sure of anything in my life, either. When Jed died, I was certain my heart and my dreams had died with him. I was so young, and had so much responsibility that I didn't think I'd ever be able to risk loving someone again." She shook her head. "I didn't ever want to go through that kind of pain again, nor did I ever want to put Rusty through it again. But then, we met you, and it seemed as if all the pain and sorrow of the past few years melted away, slowly replaced by hope and love." She snuggled closer, enjoying the comfort and safety of his arms. "I'd say we both got a wonderful deal." Katie hesitated. "Lucas?" Nuzzled against his shoulder, she glanced up at him. "Can I ask you something?"

He chuckled, tightening his arm around her. "You sound like Rusty, now. Sure, go ahead. You can ask me anything," he said, meaning it.

"Do you have…like, a favorite name for a little girl, I mean if you ever had one?"

"It's funny you should ask me that, Katie," Lucas said, kissing her forehead. "I've been thinking about that all night, about how wonderful it would be to have more children, especially a little girl."

"So do you want more children?" she asked in delight and he nodded.

"The more the merrier," he repeated her line back to her, earning a grin. "And I can't wait to get started."

"And what would you name this little girl?"

"You won't laugh?" he asked, and she shook her head.

"Promise."

"I've always kind of loved the name…Savannah."

"Savannah," Katie repeated, not in the least bit surprised. "Well sweetheart, I have a feeling your wish is about to be granted," Katie said with a laugh, putting a hand on her belly.

She'd tell him later, when she was absolutely positive she was expecting. For now, Lucas loved her and Rusty, and they were going to be a family. A real family once again.

All the yearning in her heart was gone, finally, replaced by a never-ending, unconditional love, a healing love that was both deep and inspiring.

It was what they had needed all along.

* * * * *

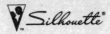

SPECIAL EDITION™

presents

the first book in a heartwarming
new series by

Kristin Hardy

Because there's
no place like home
for the holidays…

WHERE THERE'S SMOKE

(November 2005, SE#1720)

Sloane Hillyard took a very personal interest in her
work inventing fire safety equipment—after all, her
firefighter brother had died in the line of duty. And
when Boston fire captain Nick Trask signed up to
test her inventions, things got even more personal…
their mutual attraction set off alarms. But could
Sloane trust her heart to a man who risked his
life and limb day in and day out?

Available November 2005 at your favorite retail outlet.

Where love comes alive™

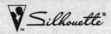

SPECIAL EDITION™

This month, Silhouette Special Edition brings
you the fifth book in the
exciting continuity

ELEVEN STUDENTS.

ONE REUNION.

AND A SECRET THAT WILL CHANGE
EVERYONE'S LIVES.

SECRETS OF A GOOD GIRL
(SE #1719)

by

Jen Safrey

Years ago, Cassidy Maxwell decided that the only way to
escape her memories was to run—as far as she could—
from everything she'd ever known. Ten years later an old
friend needs her—and a lost love wants her. Will she have
the strength to face her painful past?

**Don't miss this emotional story—
only from Silhouette Books.**

Available at your favorite retail outlet.

Where love comes alive™

COMING NEXT MONTH

#1717 THE BORROWED RING—Gina Wilkins
Family Found
Tracking down childhood friend Daniel Andreas was an assignment
close to P.I. Brittany Samples's heart. But things took an unexpected
turn when "B.J." caught her quarry—who dispensed with reunion
formalities and recruited her to pose as his wife! Soon their dangerous
new mission had B.J. wishing the husband-and-wife cover wasn't just
an act....

#1718 A MONTANA HOMECOMING—Allison Leigh
When Laurel Runyan returned to Lucius, Montana, after her estranged
father's death, she had nowhere else to go—she'd recently broken off
an engagement and given up her job and apartment. But having her first
love, sheriff Shane Golightly, as a neighbor reopened old wounds. Was
Laurel ready to give her hometown—and Shane—a second chance?

#1719 SECRETS OF A GOOD GIRL—Jen Safrey
Most Likely To...
While at Saunders University, coed Cassidy Maxwell and teaching
assistant Eric Barnes had put off romance until Cassidy got her degree.
Then she hadn't shown up at graduation, and Eric was crushed. Now,
years later, he'd gone to London to woo her back. But Cassidy wanted
to keep her childhood friend—and her own dark Saunders secrets—in
the past....

#1720 WHERE THERE'S SMOKE—Kristin Hardy
Holiday Hearts
After her brother died fighting a blaze, Sloane Hillyard took action,
inventing a monitor to improve firefighter safety. She found a reluctant
test subject in Boston fire captain Nick Trask—who warmed to the task
as his attraction for Sloane grew. But after losing her brother, would
Sloane risk her heart on another of Boston's bravest?

#1721 MARRIAGE, INTERRUPTED—Karen Templeton
Cass Stern was on edge—newly widowed, saddled with debt, running
a business and *very* pregnant. Things couldn't get weirder—until her
first husband, Blake Carter, showed up at her second husband's funeral.
Blake wanted more time with their teenaged son—and he wanted Cass
back. Cass's body screamed "Yes!" but...well, there were a lot of
buts....

#1722 WHERE HE BELONGS—Gail Barrett
For Harley-riding, smoke-jumping rebel Wade Winslow, it was
tough going back to Millstown and facing his past. But former flame
Erin McCuen and her financial troubles struck a chord with the bad
boy, so he decided to stay for a while. The stubborn and independent
woman wouldn't accept Wade's help...but could she convince him to
give their renewed passion a fighting chance?